Kelly Hunter has always had a weakness for fairy tales, fantasy worlds and losing herself in a good book. She has two children, avoids cooking and cleaning and, despite the best efforts of her family, is no sports fan. Kelly is, however, a keen gardener and has a fondness for roses. Kelly was born in Australia and has travelled extensively. Although she enjoys living and working in different parts of the world, she still calls Australia home.

Also by Kelly Hunter

Claimed by a King miniseries

Shock Heir for the Crown Prince
Convenient Bride for the King

Discover more at millsandboon.co.uk

CONVENIENT BRIDE FOR THE KING

KELLY HUNTER

MILLS & BOON

First Published in Great Britain 2018
by Mills & Boon, an imprint of HarperCollins*Publishers*
1 London Bridge Street, London, SE1 9GF

© 2018 Kelly Hunter

ISBN: 978-0-263-07559-5

MIX
Paper from
responsible sources
FSC™ C007454

This book is produced from independently certified FSC™ paper
to ensure responsible forest management.
For more information visit www.harpercollins.co.uk/green.

Printed and bound in Great Britain
by CPI Group (UK) Ltd, Croydon, CR0 4YY

CHAPTER ONE

PRINCESS MORIANA OF ARUN wasn't an unreasonable woman. She had patience aplenty and was willing to give anyone the benefit of the doubt at least once. Maybe even twice. But when she knew for a fact she was being passed around like a Christmas cracker no one wanted to pull, all bets were off.

Her brother Augustus had said he wasn't available to speak with her this morning. People to see, kingdom to rule.

Nothing to do with avoiding her until she regained her equilibrium after yesterday's spectacularly public jilting…the *coward*.

So what if Casimir of Byzenmaach no longer wanted to marry her? It wasn't as if it had ever been Casimir's idea in the first place, and it certainly hadn't been hers. When you were the progeny of kings it was commonplace for a politically expedient marriage to be arranged for you. And yet…inexplicably… Casimir's defection after such a long courtship had gutted her. He'd made her feel small and insignificant, unwanted and alone, and, above all, not good enough. All her hard work, the endless social politics, the restraint that guided her every move, had been for what?

Nothing.

Absolutely nothing.

Arun's royal palace was an austere one, mainly because Moriana's forefathers had planned it that way. Stern, grey and never quite warm enough, it invited application to duty over frivolous timewasting. It chose function over beauty, no matter how much beauty she found to hang on its walls. It favoured formal cloistered gardens for tidy minds.

Her brother had taken residence in the southern wing of the palace in the gloomiest rooms of them all, and not for the first time did Moriana wonder why. Her brother's executive secretary—an elderly courtier who'd been in service to the House of Arun since before she was born—looked up as she approached, his expression smooth and unruffled.

'Princess, what a pleasant surprise.'

She figured her appearance was neither pleasant nor a surprise, but she let the man have his social graces. 'Is he in?'

'He's taking an important call.'

'But he is in,' she countered and kept right on walking towards her brother's closed door. 'Wonderful.'

The older man sighed and pressed a button on the intercom as she swept past. He didn't actually *speak* into the intercom, mind. Moriana was pretty sure he had a secret code button set up just for her—doubtless announcing that Moriana the Red was incoming.

Her brother looked up when she walked in, told whoever he had on the phone that he'd call them back, and put the phone down.

Damn but it was cold in here. It didn't help that the spring just past had been a brutal one and summer had been slow to arrive. 'Why is it like an ice box in here?'

she asked. 'Have we no heating you can turn on? No warmer rooms you could rule from?'

'Or you could wear warmer clothes,' her brother suggested, but there was nothing wrong with her attire. Her fine wool dress was boat-necked, long-sleeved and fell to just above her knees. Stockings added another layer to her legs. She was wearing knee-high leather boots. Had she added a coat she'd be ready for a trip to the Antarctic.

'It is a perfectly pleasant day outside,' she countered. 'Why do you choose the coldest rooms we have to call your own?'

'If I had better rooms, more people would be tempted to visit me and I'd never get any work done.' His eyes were almost black and framed by thick black lashes, just like her own. His smile was indulgent as he sat back and steepled his hands—maybe his whole *I'm in charge of the universe* pose worked on some, but she'd grown up with him and knew what Augustus had looked like as a six-year-old with chickenpox and as a teenager with his first hangover. She knew the sound of his laughter and the shape of his sorrows. He could wear his kingly authority in public and she would bow to him but here in private, when it was just the two of them, he was nothing more than a slightly irritating older brother. 'What can I do for you?' he asked.

'Have you seen this?' She held up a thick sheet of cream-coloured vellum.

'Depends,' he said.

She slammed the offending letter down on the ebony desk in front of him. Letters generally didn't slam down on anything but this one had the weight of her hand behind it. 'Theo sent me a proposal.'

'Okay,' he said cautiously, still looking at her rather than the letter.

'A *marriage* proposal.'

Her brother's lips twitched.

'Don't you dare,' she warned.

'Well, it stands to reason he would,' said Augustus. 'You're available, he's under increasing pressure to produce an heir and secure the throne, and politically it's an opportunistic match.'

'We loathe each other. There is no earthly reason why Theo would want to spend an evening with me, let alone eternity.'

'I have a theory about that—'

'Don't start.'

'It goes something like this. He pulled your pigtail when you were children, you gave him a black eye and you've been fierce opponents ever since. If you actually spent some time with the man you'd discover he's not half as bad as you think he is. He's well-travelled, well-read, surprisingly intelligent and a consummate negotiator. All things you admire.'

'A consummate negotiator? Are you serious? Theo's marriage proposal is a *form* letter. He filled my name in at the top and his at the bottom.'

'And he has a sense of humour,' Augustus said.

'Says who?'

'Everyone except for you.'

'Doesn't that tell you something?'

'Yes.'

Oh, it was *on*.

She pulled up a chair, a hard unwelcoming one because that was all there was to be had in this farce of a room. She sat. He sighed. She crossed her legs, etiquette be damned. Two seconds later she uncrossed her legs, rearranged her skirt over her knees and sat ram-rod-straight as she stared him down. 'Did you arrange this?' Because she wouldn't put it past him. He and their three neighbouring monarchs were close. They plotted together on a regular basis.

'Me? No.'

'Did Casimir?' He of the broken matrimonial intentions and newly discovered offspring.

'I doubt it. What with burying his father and planning a coronation, the instant fatherhood and his current wooing of the child's mother... I'm pretty sure he has his hands full.'

Moriana drummed her fingers on his ugly wooden desk, partly because it gave her time to digest her brother's words and partly because she knew it annoyed him. 'Then whose mad idea was it?'

He eyed her offending fingers for a moment before casually pulling open his desk drawer and pulling out a long wooden ruler. He held it up, as if gauging its reach, before bringing the tip to rest gently in his palm. 'Stop torturing my desk.'

'Or you'll beat me? Please,' she scoffed. Nonetheless, she stopped with the drumming and brought the offending hand in front of her to examine her nails. No damage at all. Maybe she'd paint her nails black later, to match the desk and her mood. Maybe her rebellion could start small. 'You haven't answered my question. Whose idea was it?'

'I'm assuming it was Theo's.'

She looked up to find Augustus eyeing her steadily, as if he knew something she didn't.

'It's not an insult, Moriana; it's an honour. You were born and raised for the kind of position Theo's offering.

You could make a difference to his leadership and to the stability of the region.'

'No.' She cut him off fast. 'You can't guilt me into this. I am *through* with being the good princess who does what she's told, the one who serves and serves and *serves,* without any thought to my own needs. I'm going to Cannes to party up a scandal. There will be recklessness. Orgies with dissolute film stars.'

'When?' Augustus did not sound alarmed.

'Soon.' He didn't *look* alarmed either, and he should have. 'You don't think I'll do it. You think I'm a humourless prude who wouldn't know fun times if they rained down on me. Well, they're about to. I want the passion of a lover's touch. I want a man to look at me with lust. Dammit, for once in my life I want to do something that pleases *me!*' She'd had enough. 'All those things I've been taught to place value on? My reputation, my sense of duty to king and country, my virginity? I'm getting rid of them.'

'Okay, let's not be hasty.'

'Hasty?' Princesses didn't screech. Moriana dropped her voice an octave and gave it some gravel instead. 'I could have had the stable boy when I was eighteen. He was beautiful, carefree and rode like a demon. At twenty-two I could have had a sheikh worth billions. He only had to look at me to make me melt. A year later I met a musician with hands I could only dream of. I would have gladly taken him to my bed but I *didn't.* Would you like me to continue?'

'*Please* don't.'

'Casimir's not a virgin,' she continued grimly. '*He* got a nineteen-year-old pregnant when he was twenty-three! You know what I was doing at twenty-three? Taking dancing lessons so that I could feel the touch of someone's hand.'

'I thought they were fencing lessons.'

'Same thing. Maybe I wanted to feel a little prick.' All these years she'd denied herself all manner of pleasures others took for granted. 'I have *waited*. No romance, no lovers, no children for Moriana of Arun. Only duty. And for what? So that today I could wake up and be vilified in the press for being too cool, too stern and too focused on fundraising and furthering my education to have time for any man? I mean, no wonder Casimir of Byzenmaach went looking for someone else, right?'

Augustus winced. 'No one's saying that.'

'Have you even read today's newspapers?'

'No one *here* is saying that,' he amended.

'What did I do wrong, Augustus? I was promised to an indifferent boy when I was eight years old. Now I'm getting a form letter marriage proposal from a playboy king whose dislike for me is legendary. And you say I should feel honoured?' Her voice cracked. 'Why do you sell me off so *easily*? Am I really that worthless?'

She straightened her shoulders, smoothed her hands over the skirt of her dress and made sure the hem sat in a straight stern line. She hated losing her composure, hated feeling needy and greedy and hard to love. She was wired to please others. Trained to it since birth.

But this…expecting her to fall all over herself to comply with Theo's request… 'Theo's uncle is making waves again and questioning Theo's fitness to rule. I do read the reports that come in.' She read every last one of them. 'I understand Liesendaach's need for stability and a secure future and that we in Arun would rather deal with Theo than with his uncle. But I am *not* the solution to his need for a quickie marriage.'

'Actually, you're an excellent solution.' Augustus was watching her carefully. 'You've been looking forward to having a family for years. Theo needs an heir. You could be pregnant within a year.'

'Don't.' Yes, she wanted children. She'd foolishly once thought she'd be married with several children by now.

'You and Theo have goals that align. I'm merely stating the obvious.'

Moriana wrapped her arms around her waist and stared at the toes of her boots. The boots were a shade darker than the purple of her dress. The pearls around her neck matched the pearls in her ears. She was a picture-perfect princess who was falling apart inside. 'Maybe I don't want children any more. Maybe keeping royal children safe and happy and feeling loved is an impossible task.'

'Our parents seemed to manage it well enough.'

'Oh, really?' She knew she should hold her tongue. She didn't, and all her years of trying and failing to please people bubbled to the fore. 'Do you think I feel loved? By whom?' She choked on a laugh. 'You, who would just as soon trade me into yet another loveless marriage in return for regional stability? Casimir, who never wanted me in the first place and was simply too gutless to say so? Theo, with his form letter marriage proposal and endless parade of mistresses? Do you really think I've basked in the glow of unconditional parental love and approval for the past twenty-eight years? Heaven help me, Augustus. What *planet* are you living on? Not one of you even remembers I exist unless I can *do* something for you.'

She felt stupid. Stupid for putting her life on hold for a decade and never once calling into question that childhood betrothal. She could have asked for a time frame from Casimir. She could have pressed for a solid commitment. She could have said no to many things and got over trying to please people who didn't give a damn about her. She gestured towards Theo's offending letter. 'He doesn't even *pretend* to offer love or attraction. Not even mild affection.'

'Is that what you want?'

'Yes! I want to be with someone who cares for me. Why is that so hard to understand?'

'Maybe he does.'

'What?'

'Theo. Maybe he cares for you.'

'You don't seriously expect me to believe that.' Moriana looked at him in amazement. 'You do. Oh. You must think I'm really stupid.'

'It's a theory.'

'Would you like me to disprove it for you?' Because she had years and years of dealing with Theo to call on. 'I can count on one hand the times I've felt that man's support. The first was at our mother's funeral when he caught me as I stumbled on the steps of the church. He made me sit before I fell. He brought me water and sat with me in silence and kept his hatred of women wearing black to himself. The second and final time he was supportive of me was at a regional water summit when a drunk delegate put his hand on my backside. Theo told him he'd break it if it wasn't removed.'

'I like it,' said her brother with a faint smile.

'You would.'

'He knows where you are in a room full of people,' Augustus said next. 'He always knows. He can describe whatever it is you're wearing.'

'So he's observant.'

'It's more than that.'

'I disagree. Maybe he's wanted me a time or two,

I'll give him that. But only for sport, and only because he couldn't have me.' She plucked the form letter from the desk and folded it so that the offending words were hidden. 'No, Augustus. It's a smart offer. Theo's a smart man. I can see exactly what kind of political gain is in it for him. But there's nothing in it for me. Nothing I want.'

'I hear you,' Augustus replied quietly.

'Good.' She sent her brother a tight smile. 'Maybe I'll send a form letter refusal. *Dear Applicant, After careful consideration I regret to inform you that your proposal has been unsuccessful. Better luck next time.'*

'That would be inviting him to try again. This is Theo, remember?'

'You're right.' Moriana reconsidered her words. *'Better luck elsewhere?'*

'Yes.' Her brother smiled but his eyes remained clouded with concern. 'Moriana—'

'Don't,' she snapped. 'Don't you try and guilt me into doing this.'

'I'm not. You're free to choose. Free to be. Free to discover who and what makes you happy.'

'Good. Good chat. I should bare my soul to you more often.'

Augustus shuddered.

Moriana rounded her brother's imposing desk and kissed the top of his head, mainly because she knew such a blatant display of affection would irritate him. 'I'm sorry,' she whispered. 'I like what Theo's doing for his country. I applaud the progress and stability he's bringing to the region and I want it to continue. There's plenty to admire about him these days, and if I thought he actually liked me or that there was any chance he could meet my needs I'd marry him and make the most of it. I don't need to be swept off my feet. But this time I *do* want attention and affection and fidelity in return for my service. Love even, heaven forbid. And that's not Theo's wheelhouse.'

Augustus, reigning King of Arun and brother to Moriana the Red, watched as his sister turned on her boot heel and headed for the door.

'Moriana.' It was easier to talk to her retreating form than say it to her face. 'I do love you, you know. I want you to be happy.'

Her step faltered, but she didn't look back as she closed the door behind her.

Augustus, worst brother in the world, put his hands to his face and breathed deeply before reaching for the phone on his desk.

He didn't know, he couldn't be sure if Theo had stayed on the line or not, but still…the option to do so had been there.

Mistake.

He picked up the phone and listened for a moment but there was only silence. 'You still there?' he asked finally.

'Yes.'

Damn. 'I wish you hadn't heard that.'

'She's magnificent.' A thousand miles away, King Theodosius of Liesendaach let out a breath and ran a hand through his short-cropped hair. He had the fair hair and blue-grey eyes of his forefathers, the build of a warrior and no woman had ever refused him. Until now. He didn't know whether to be insulted or to applaud. 'The stable boy? Really?'

'I wish *I* hadn't heard that.' Augustus sounded weary. 'What the hell are you doing, sending her a form letter marriage proposal? I thought you wanted her co-operation.'

'I do want her co-operation. I will confess, I wasn't expecting quite that much *no* in response.'

'You thought she'd fall all over the offer.'

'I thought she'd at least consider it.'

'She did.' Augustus's tone was dry—very dry. 'When's the petition for your removal from the throne being tabled?'

'Week after next, assuming my uncle gets the support he needs. He's close.' The petition was based on a clause in Liesendaach's constitution that enabled a monarch who had no intention of marrying and producing an heir to be removed from the throne. The clause hadn't been enforced in over three hundred years.

'You need a plan B,' said Augustus.

'I have a plan B. It involves talking to your sister in person.'

'You heard her. She's not interested.'

'Stable boy,' Theo grated. 'Dissolute film star. Would you rather she took up with them?'

'Why are you any more worthy? A damn *form letter*, Theo.' Augustus appeared to be working up to a snit of his own. 'Couldn't you have at least shown up? I thought you cared for her. I honestly thought you cared for her more than you ever let on, otherwise I would have never encouraged this.'

'I do care for her.' She was everything a future queen of Liesendaach should be. Poised, competent, politically aware and beautiful. Very, *very* beautiful. He'd dragged his heels for years when it came to providing Liesendaach with a queen.

And now Moriana, Princess of Arun, was free.

Her anger at her current situation had nothing on Theo's when he thought of how much *time* they'd wasted. '*Your sister* put herself on hold for a man who didn't want her, and you—first as her brother, and then as her King—did nothing to either expedite or dissolve that commitment. All those years she spent sidelined and waiting. All her hard-won self-confidence dashed by polite indifference. Do you care for her? Has Casimir *ever* given a damn? Because from where I sit, neither of you could have cared for her any *less*. I may not love her the way she wants to be loved. Frankly, I don't love anyone like that and never have. But at least I notice her *existence*.'

Silence from the King of Arun.

'You miscalculated with the form letter,' Augustus said finally.

'So it would seem,' Theo gritted out.

'I advise you to let her cool down before you initiate any further contact.'

'No. Why do you never let your sister run hot?' Even as a child he'd hated seeing Moriana's fiery spirit squashed beneath the weight of royal expectations. And, later, it was one of the reasons he fought with her so much. Not the only one—sexual frustration had also played its part. But when he and Moriana clashed, her fire stayed lit. He *liked* that.

'I need to see her.' Theo ran a hand through his already untidy hair. 'I'm not asking you to speak with her on my behalf. I've already heard you do exactly that and, by the way, thanks for nothing. What kind of diplomat are you? Yes, I'm being pressured to marry and produce heirs. That's not an argument I would have led with.'

'I didn't lead with it. I mentioned it in passing. I also sang your praises and pushed harder than I should have on your behalf. You're welcome.'

'I can give her what she wants. Affection, attention, even fidelity.'

Not love, but you couldn't have everything.

'That's your assessment. It's not hers.'

'I need to speak with her.'

'No,' said Augustus. 'You need to grovel.'

CHAPTER TWO

PUBLIC FLAYING OR NOT, Moriana's charity commitments continued throughout the day and into the evening. She'd put together a charity antique art auction for the children's hospital months ago and the event was due to start at six p.m. in one of the palace function rooms that had been set up for the occasion. The auctioneers had been in residence all day, setting up the display items. Palace staff were on duty to take care of the catering, security was in place and there was no more work to be done beyond turning up, giving a speech and subtly persuading some of the region's wealthiest inhabitants to part with some of their excess money. Moriana was good at hosting such events. Her mother had taught her well.

Not that Moriana had ever managed to live up to those exacting standards when her mother was alive. It had taken years of dogged, determined practice to even reach her current level of competence.

The principality of Arun wasn't the wealthiest principality in the region. That honour went to Byzenmaach, ruled by Casimir, her former intended. It also wasn't the prettiest. Theo's Liesendaach was far prettier, embellished by centuries of rulers who'd built civic buildings and public spaces beyond compare. No, Arun's claim to fame lay in its healthcare and education systems, and this was due in no small measure to her ceaseless work in those areas, and her mother's and grandmother's attention before that. Rigidly repressed the women of the royal house of Arun might be but they knew how to champion the needs of their people.

Tonight would be an ordeal. The press had not been kind to her today and she'd tried to put that behind her and carry on as usual. The main problem being that *no one else* was carrying on as usual. Even Aury, her unflappable lady-in-waiting, had been casting anxious glances in Moriana's direction all day.

Moriana's favourite treat, lemon tart with a burnt sugar top, had been waiting for her at morning tea, courtesy of the palace kitchens. A vase full of fat pink peonies had been sitting on her sideboard by lunchtime. She'd caught one of her publicity aides mid-rant on the phone—he'd been threatening to revoke someone's palace press pass if they ran a certain headline, and he'd flushed when he'd seen her but he'd kept right on making threats until he'd got his way.

There'd been a certain lack of newspapers in the palace this morning, which meant that Moriana had had to go online to read them.

She should have stayed away.

There was this game she and her lady-in-waiting often made out of the news of the day. While Aury styled Moriana's hair for whatever function was on that evening, they'd shoot headlines back and forth. On a normal day it encouraged analysis and discussion.

On a normal day the headlines wouldn't be proclaiming Moriana the most undesirable princess on the planet.

'Too Cold to Wed,' Moriana said as Aury reached for the pins that would secure Moriana's braid into an elegant roll at the base of her head.

'No,' said Aury, pointing a stern hairbrush in the direction of Moriana's reflection. 'I'm not doing this today and neither are you. I stopped reading them so I wouldn't choke on my breakfast, and you should have stopped reading them too.'

'Jilted Ice Princess Contemplates Nunnery,' Moriana continued.

'I'm not coming with you to the nunnery. They don't care what hair looks like there, the heathens,' said Aury, pushing a hairpin into place. 'Okay, no, I will give you a headline. *Byzenmaach Mourns as the Curse Strikes Again.'*

'Curse?' Moriana had missed that one. 'What curse?'

'Apparently you refused to marry King Casimir in an attempt to avoid the same fate as his mother. Namely, being physically, mentally and verbally abused by your husband for years before taking a lover, giving birth to your lover's child, seeing both killed by your husband and then committing suicide.'

'Ouch.' Moriana caught her lady-in-waiting's gaze in the mirror. 'What paper was that?'

'A regional one from Byzenmaach's northern border. The *Mountain Chronicle.*'

'Vultures.' Never mind that she'd accidentally overheard her parents discussing a remarkably similar scenario involving Casimir's parents. She'd never repeated the conversation to anyone but Augustus and she never would. 'Casimir doesn't deserve that one.'

'Byzenmaach Monarch Faces Backlash over Secret Lover and Child,' said Aury next.

'That one I like. Serves him right. Do we have the run sheet for the auction tonight?'

'It's right here. And the guest list.'

Moriana scanned through the paperwork Aury

handed her. 'Augustus is attending now and bringing a guest? He didn't say anything about it to me this morning.'

Not that she'd given him a chance to say anything much. Still.

'Word came through from his office this afternoon. Also, Lord and Lady Curtis send their apologies. Their granddaughter had a baby this afternoon.'

'Have we sent our congratulations?'

'We have.'

'Tell the auctioneer to put my reserve on the baby bear spoon set. They can have it as a gift.' Arun might not be the wealthiest or the prettiest kingdom in the region but its people did not go unattended.

'I put the silver gown out for tonight, along with your grandmother's diamonds. I also took the liberty of laying out the blood-red gown you love but never wear and the pearl choker and earrings from the royal collection. The silver gown is a perfectly appropriate choice, don't get me wrong, but I for one am hoping the Ice Princess might feel like making a statement tonight.'

'And you think a red gown and a to-hell-with-you-all attitude will do this?'

'It beats looking whipped.'

'The red gown it is,' Moriana murmured. The Ice Princess was overdue for a thaw. 'Now all I need is a wholly inappropriate date to go with it.' She took a deep breath and let it out slowly. 'Actually, no. I'm not so merciless as to drag anyone else into this mess. I'll go alone.'

'You'll not be alone for long,' Aury predicted. 'Opportunists will flock to you.'

'It's already started.'

'Anyone you like?'

'No.' Moriana ignored the sudden image of a harshly

hewn face and glittering grey eyes. 'Well, Theo. Who I've never actually tried to like. It never seemed worth the effort.'

Aury stopped fussing with Moriana's hair in favour of looking stunned. 'Theodosius of Liesendaach is courting you now?'

'I wouldn't call it courting.' Moriana thought back to the form letter and scowled. 'Trust me, neither would anyone else.'

'Yes, but *really*?'

'Aury, your tongue is hanging out.'

'Uh huh. Have you *seen* that man naked?'

'Oh, yes. God bless the paparazzi. *Everyone* has seen that man naked.'

'And what a treat it was.'

Okay, so he was well endowed. And reputedly very skilled in the bedroom. Women did not complain of him. Old lovers stayed disconcertingly friendly with him.

'You'd take me to Liesendaach with you, right?' asked Aury as she started in on Moriana's hair again, securing the roll with pearl-tipped pins and leaving front sections of hair loose to be styled into soft curls. 'I can start packing any time. Say the word. I am there for you. Of course, I am also here for you.' Aury sighed heavily.

'You should have pursued a career in drama,' Moriana said. 'Arun's not so bad. A little austere at times. A little grey around the edges. And at the centre. But there's beauty here too, if you know where to look.'

'I know where to look.' Aury sighed afresh. 'And clearly so does Theodosius of Liesendaach. Be careful with that one.'

'I can handle Theo.'

Aury looked uncommonly troubled, her dark eyes wary and her lips tilted towards a frown. 'He strikes me as a man who gets what he wants. What if he decides he wants you?'

'He doesn't. Theo's been reliably antagonistic towards me since childhood. And when he's not prodding me with a pointy stick he's totally indifferent to my presence. He's just…going through the motions. Being a casual opportunist. If I turn him down he'll go away.'

Aury sighed again and Moriana could feel a lecture coming on. Aury had several years on Moriana, not enough to make her a mother figure, but more than enough to fulfil the role of older, wiser sister. It was a role she took seriously.

'My lady, as one woman to another… Okay, as one slightly more experienced woman to another…please don't be taken in by Theodosius of Liesendaach's apparent indifference to events and people that surround him. That man is like a hawk in a granary. He's watching, he's listening and he knows what he wants from any given situation. More to the point, he knows what *everyone else* wants from any given situation.'

'He doesn't know what I want.'

'Want to bet?' Aury sounded uncommonly serious. 'Yes, he's charming, he's playful, he's extremely good at acting as if he couldn't care less. But what else do we know of him? Think about it. We know that for the first fifteen years of his life he never expected to be King. We know that for ten years after the death of his parents and brother he watched and waited his turn while his uncle bled Liesendaach dry as Regent. *The young Crown Prince is indifferent to our plight*, the people said. *He's bad blood, too busy pleasing himself to care about the rape of our country*, they said. *We can't look to him to save us. He will not bring an end to this.* That's what his uncle thought. It's what everyone thought. It's what he wanted them to think.'

Aury reached for another pin. 'Do you remember the day Theodosius of Liesendaach turned twenty-five and took the throne? I do. Because from that day forward he systematically destroyed his uncle and squashed every last parasite. He targeted their every weakness, he knew exactly where to strike, and he has fought relentlessly to bring his country back to prosperity. That's not indifference. That's patience, planning, ruthless execution and fortitude. He was *never* indifferent to his country's plight. I don't trust that man's *indifference* one little bit.'

'Point taken.'

'I hope so.' Aury finished with Moriana's hair and pulled the make-up trolley closer. She rifled through the lipstick drawer and held up a blood-red semi-gloss for inspection. 'What else are we thinking?'

'I'm thinking smoky eyes and lipstick one shade lighter. It's a charity auction, not a nightclub.'

'Boring,' said Aury.

'Baby steps.' Moriana had already chosen a dress she wasn't entirely comfortable with.

Aury found a lighter shade of lipstick and held it up for inspection. 'What about this one?'

'Yes.' Aury rarely steered her wrong. 'And Aury?'

'Yes, milady?'

'I'll be careful.'

Augustus was a deceitful, manipulative son of Satan, Moriana decided when he stepped into the auction room later that evening with his *guest* in tow. It wasn't a woman. Oh, no. Her brother hadn't done anything so lacklustre as bringing a suitable date with him to the event. Instead, he'd brought a neighbouring monarch along for the ride. Theo, to be more precise. He of the hawkish grace, immaculate dinner suit and form letter marriage proposal.

Theo and Augustus had been thick as thieves as children. They'd grown apart in their teens when Theo had flung himself headlong into reckless debauchery after the death of his family. Augustus had only followed him so far before their father, the then monarch of Arun, had reined him in. Theo had experienced no such constraints. Lately though…now that Theo bore the full brunt of the Liesendaach Crown… Moriana didn't quite know what kind of relationship Theo and her brother had. They'd been working together on a regional water plan. They trusted each other's judgement in such matters. They still didn't socialise together.

Much.

That they were socialising now, the same day she'd refused Theo's offer, spoke volumes for Augustus's support of the man.

So much for blood being thicker than brotherhood.

She turned away fast when she caught her brother's gaze because this betrayal, on top of Casimir's rejection, on top of Theo's demeaning form letter, almost brought her to her knees. So much for men and all their fine promises. You couldn't trust any of them.

The chief press advisor for the palace appeared at her side, his eyes sharp but his smile in place. 'Your Highness, you look pale. May I get you anything?'

'How about a brand-new day?' she suggested quietly. 'This one's rotten, from the core out.'

'Tomorrow will be a better day,' he said.

'Promises.' Her voice was light but her heart was heavy.

'I promise we're doing our best to shine the brightest light we can on everything you do for us, milady. The entire team is on it. No one dismisses our princess lightly. No one has earned that right.'

'Thank you, Giles.' She blinked back rapid tears and looked away. 'I appreciate your support.'

And then two more people joined them. One was Theo and the other one was Augustus. Years of burying her feelings held her in good stead as she plastered a smile on her face and set about greeting them.

'Your Majesties,' she said, curtseying to them, and something of her hurt must have shown on her face as she rose because Augustus frowned and started to say something. Whatever it was, she didn't want to hear it. 'What a surprise.'

'A pleasant one, I hope,' said Theo as he took her gloved hand and lifted it to his lips.

'Oh, we all live in hope,' she offered. 'I live in hope that one day the people I hold dear will have my back, but that day's not here yet.'

'Yes, it is; you just can't see it,' Theo countered. 'I'm here, welcome or not, with the ulterior motive of being seen with you in public.'

'Indeed, I can see the headlines now. *Ice Princess Falls for Playboy King. Liesendaach Gives It a Week.*'

'Perhaps.' Theo didn't discount it. 'Or I can give your publicity officer here a quote about how much respect I have for you as a person and as a representative of the royal family of Arun. I can mention that it's no hardship whatsoever to continue to offer you my friendship, admiration and support. I can add that I'm not at all dismayed that you're now free of your ridiculous childhood betrothal to the new King of Byzenmaach. And we can see how that goes down.'

The press advisor melted away with a nod in Theo's direction. Theo and her brother stayed put.

'Damage control, Moriana. Look it up,' Theo said curtly.

'Well, I guess you'd know all about that.'

'I do.' But he didn't defend his wild past or the chaos he occasionally still stirred. He never did. Theodosius of Liesendaach didn't answer to anyone.

A small—very tiny—part of her respected that.

'So,' she said. 'Welcome to my annual Children's Hospital Charity Auction. Have you seen the catalogue?'

'I have not.'

'I'll have one sent over.' She nodded towards some nearby display cases. 'By all means, look around. You might see something you like.'

'You won't accompany me?'

'No, I'm working.' He'd dressed immaculately, as usual. No one wore a suit quite the way Theo did. He was broad-shouldered and slim-hipped. Tall enough to look down on almost everyone in the room. His cropped blond hair was nothing remarkable and his face was clean-shaven. It wasn't a pretty face. A little too stern and altogether too craggy. Lips that knifed towards cruel when he was in a bad mood. His eyes were his best feature by far. She might as well give the devil his due. They were icy blue-grey and often coolly amused. They were amused now.

'I have other duties to attend and people to greet,' she continued bluntly. 'How fortunate Augustus is here to take care of you. What a good friend.'

'Indeed he is.' Theo's gaze had yet to leave hers. 'I like it when you wear red. The colour suits you and so do the pearls. My compliments to your wardrobe mistress.'

'I'll be sure to let her know. I mean, it's not as if I

could ever be in charge of my own clothing choices, right? Who knows what I'd come up with?' There was something different about Theo tonight. Something fierce and implacable and hungry. She bared her teeth right back at him. 'Any other underhand compliments you'd like to shower me with before I take my leave?'

Augustus winced. 'Moria—'

'No!' She cut him off. 'You don't get to diminish me either. All your fine talk this morning of supporting my decisions, of letting me be. I believed you. Yet here we are.'

'Your brother's not at fault,' Theo said smoothly. 'Moriana, we need to talk.'

'About your proposal? My reply is in the mail, seeing as that's your preferred method of communication. Seeing as you're here, I dare say I can give you the highlights. I refuse. It's not you, it's me. Or maybe it is you and all those other women I'd have to live up to, I don't know. Either way, my answer's no. I am done listening to the two-faced, self-serving babble of kings. Now, if you'll both excuse me.'

'Go. Greet your guests. We can talk after you're done here. I'll wait,' said Theo the Magnanimous. 'I'm good at waiting.'

Moriana laughed. She couldn't help it. 'Theo, you may have waited for your crown but you've never waited on a woman in your life.'

She was close enough to see his jaw clench. Close enough to see hot temper flare in those eyes that ran more towards grey tonight than blue. 'Oh, Princess. Always so *wrong*.'

It wasn't easy to turn away from the challenge in his gaze but she did it, more mindful than ever of Aury's warning. This wasn't the boy she remembered from childhood or the teenager who'd poked and prodded at her until she'd snapped back. This was the man who'd watched and waited for ten long years before rising and taking his country back. This was the hawk in the granary.

And maybe, just maybe, she was the mouse.

Fifteen minutes later, after personally greeting all the guests in attendance and seeing that they were well lubricated, Moriana looked for Theo again. Not that she had to look hard. She always knew where Theo was in a room, just as she always tracked where her security detail was, and where her brother was. It was an awareness that would have made a seasoned soldier proud and she'd been trained for it since birth.

Know your exits. Know where your support is. Know where your loved ones are at any given moment. Theo wasn't a loved one but he'd always been included in that equation for he'd been a treasured child of royalty too. The last of his line and therefore important.

Casimir, her former intended, had also been the last of his line and she'd always tracked his whereabouts too, whenever they'd been at functions together. She'd misplaced Casimir on occasion—no one was perfect. She'd misplaced him on several occasions.

Many occasions.

Moving on.

Theo didn't look up from the display he was browsing as she made her way to his side. He didn't look up even as he began to speak. 'You're good at this,' he said.

'Thank you.' She wanted to believe he could pay her a genuine compliment, not that he ever had before. 'I've been hosting this particular fundraiser for the past seven years and I have it down to a fine art, pardon the pun. Collecting the auction items, curating the guest list, knowing what people want and what they'll pay to have it. Knowing who else they might want to see socially. People say I have a knack for fundraising, as if I simply fling things together at the last minute and hope for the best, but I don't. I put a lot of work into making sure these evenings flow like water and do what they're meant to do.'

'I don't doubt it,' he said, finally turning his gaze on her. 'Hence the compliment.' He tilted his head a fraction. 'You're an exceptional ambassador for your people and you'd have been an exceptional asset to Casimir as queen consort. It's Byzenmaach's loss.'

He wasn't the first person to say that to her tonight and he probably wouldn't be the last. 'I doubt Casimir's feeling any loss.' She didn't like how thready she sounded. As if she'd been stretched too thin for far too long.

'He hurt you.' Three simple words that cracked her wide open.

'Don't. Theo, please. Leave it alone. It's done.'

She turned away, suddenly wanting to get away from the sedate auction room and the gossip and the expectations that came with being a Princess of Arun. Perfect composure, always. Unrivalled social graces. A memory trained to remember names and faces. She had a welcome speech to give in fifteen minutes. Who would give it if she walked out?

He stopped her before she'd taken a step. The subtle shift of his body and the force of his silent appraisal blocked her retreat. 'You're not coping,' he said quietly. 'Tell me what you need.'

She didn't know why his softly spoken words hurt so much, but they did. 'Damn you, Theo. Don't do this to me. Don't be attentive all of a sudden because you want something from me. Do what you usually do. Fight. Snarl. Be you. Give me something I know how to respond to.'

He stilled, his face a granite mask, and she had the sudden, inexplicable feeling she'd just dealt him a brutal blow. And then his gaze cut away from her face and he took a deep breath and when he looked at her again he wore a fierce and reckless smile she knew all too well. 'I'll fight you mentally, physically, whatever you need, until we both bleed,' he promised, his voice a vicious caress. 'Just as soon as you stop *breaking* in front of me. I know your family trained you to hide weakness better than this. It's what you do. It's all you do. So do it.'

Yes. This was what she needed from him, and to hell with why. No one said she was the most well-balanced princess in the universe.

Thread by thread she pulled herself together, drawing on the anger she sensed in him to bolster her own. *Build a wall—any wall.* Anger, righteous indignation, icy disdain, attention to duty, whatever it took to keep the volcano of feelings in check.

'Have you seen the Vermeer?' she asked finally, when she had herself mostly back under control. 'I thought of you when it first came in. It would round out Liesendaach's Dutch collection.'

He studied her for what felt like hours, before nodding, as if she'd do, and then held out his arm for her to claim. 'All right, Princess. Persuade me.'

Moriana carved out the time to show Theo the most interesting pieces in the auction. She made her speech and the auction began. And by the end of the evening a great deal of money had been raised for the new children's hospital wing and Theo had almost purchased the Vermeer for a truly staggering sum. In the end the painting had gone to a gallery and Moriana dearly hoped they needed a tax write-down soon because they clearly hadn't done their sums. That or they *really* wanted to support the children's hospital.

'I thought you'd lost your mind,' she said when only a handful of guests remained and he came to congratulate her on the evening's success. 'Not even you could justify that amount of money for a lesser Vermeer.'

'But for you I tried.'

His smile reminded her of young boys and frog ponds and sultry, still evenings, back when Theo's parents had still been alive. Augustus had always caught his frogs with quick efficiency and, once examined, had let them go. Theo, on the other hand, had revelled in the chase. He'd been far more interested in which way they jumped and where they might try to hide than in actually catching them. To this day, Moriana didn't know what that said about either Theo or her brother.

'Are you ready for that drink yet?' he asked.

'What drink?'

'The one we're going to have tonight, when you graciously reconsider my proposal.'

'Oh, *that* drink. We're not having that drink any time soon. You're getting a form letter rejection in the post, remember?'

'You wouldn't.'

'I did. You'll receive it tomorrow, unless you're still here. I assume Augustus has offered you palace hospitality?'

Theo inclined his head.

Of course. 'Then perhaps you should find him. I'm about to retire for the evening.'

'You said you'd give me five minutes of your time.'

'I said nothing of the sort. And yet here I am. Giving you my time.' If she'd worn a watch she'd have glanced at it.

'I gave you a fight when you needed one earlier.' Since when had his voice been able to lick at her like flames? 'I didn't want to, but I did. Here's what I want in return. One kiss. Here or in private. Put your hands on me, just once. You have my permission. I'll even keep mine to myself. And if you don't like touching and kissing me I'll withdraw my pursuit at once. Does that not sound fair and honest? Am I being unjust?'

Gone was the teasing menace of her childhood and the reckless philanderer of her youth. In their place stood a man in pursuit, confident and dangerous.

He'd been waiting for her when she'd finished her speech, approval in his eyes and a glass of champagne in hand that he handed to *her*. Faultlessly attentive. Silently supportive.

Tell me what you need.

A fight. A snarl. Barbed compliments. His attention. Something other than rejection to focus on.

'One drink. One kiss,' he murmured. 'Do you need to collect a coat of some sort? Because I'm ready to leave.'

'Why would I leave with you? Why would I indulge you in this?'

'Because I have something you want. Several somethings.'

'No, you don't. If you had anything I wanted, I'd be giving your proposal all due consideration.'

'Position.' His eyes never left her face.

'Yawn.' She was Princess of Arun.

'Passion. You've never felt it but you want it, nonetheless.'

'Maybe.' She was honest enough to concede his point. 'But you're not the only man to inspire passion in a woman. Plenty do. I can find passion without you.'

His eyes flashed silver.

'Temper, *temper*,' she said.

'Commitment,' he offered next.

'We all exercise that. I'm already committed to various causes, not to mention my country and my family. Some would say I'm blindly overcommitted to many things and receive little in return, and they're probably right. Commitment is overrated.'

His eyes never left her face. 'Commitment to you.'

CHAPTER THREE

HE WAS GOOD at this. Aury had warned her. He knew
exactly what to offer in order to make her heart thump
with painful hope and longing.

'Let's talk about this somewhere without the avid audience,' he muttered.

She glanced beyond him discreetly, only to realise he
was right. Those who had yet to leave seemed to have
no intention of doing so with her and Theo putting on
a show right in front of their eyes. Even Augustus was
staring at them, his eyes full of clear warning.

*Don't make a spectacle of yourself. Remember your
place.*

Don't embarrass me.

Don't make me regret that we're related.

'Five minutes,' she said to Theo, as she nodded mi-
nutely at her brother—*message received*—and headed
for the door.

Moriana lived in a wing of the royal palace. She'd
furnished it to her taste, raided the palace's art collection until she was satisfied with the result and had purchased whatever pieces she felt were missing. Augustus
could complain about her spending—and he did—but
her ledger was in the black.

In the space of five years she'd tripled the value of

the royal art collection and outlaid only a fraction of that cost. She wheeled and dealed, had an eye for a bargain and the sensibilities of a curator. And, of course, she had the throne of Arun behind her.

She had dual degrees in politics and fine arts. Connections the world over. She was the ambassador for a dozen different charities and she took those roles seriously. She was educated, accomplished and blessed with favourable looks, or so she'd been told. She was in a position to make a difference.

And nervous. Dear heaven, she was nervous as Theo prowled around her sitting room, staring at her furnishings and possessions as if they held secrets he wanted to know.

'You wanted a drink?' she asked.

'If you're having one.' He put his hands in his trouser pockets and continued to study the sculpture on a small side table. 'It's fake,' he said of the copied Rodin.

'I know. But it's a good copy and it's still very beautiful.' She'd paid a pittance for it. 'How do you know it's a fake?' Not many would. Not without examining it thoroughly, and he hadn't.

'Because my father gifted the real one to my mother on their tenth wedding anniversary.'

Oh, well. There you go. 'I have Scotch.'

'Perfect.'

She poured him a serve and then doubled it because it wouldn't do to have her serve be twice the size of his.

He was standing by the fireplace and she crossed the room with all the grace she could muster and handed him the drink.

'I like this room,' he said. 'It's more comfortable than I thought it would be.'

'I use it,' she said simply, and tried not to look at his

lips but they were impossible to ignore now that he'd put the idea of kissing into her head. 'I like jewel colours and textured fabrics. I like comfortable furniture.'

'Your taste is exquisite.' He sipped his drink. 'Does Augustus know you serve his special Scotch?'

'Does he need to know?' she countered. 'Because, frankly, he's slightly precious about it.' She took a sip of hers. 'You sent me a form letter proposal.'

'I had it specially made just for you.'

'Now you're making fun of me.'

'Not really. The scions of the House of Liesendaach always put their marriage proposals in writing. It's the rule.'

Byzenmaach didn't have such a rule and neither did Arun. Her and Casimir's engagement had been more of a verbal agreement between their parents than anything she'd signed up for. Maybe there was some small merit to Theo's form letter after all.

'A marriage proposal is usually accompanied by a ring,' she said. There'd never been one of those between her and Casimir either.

Theo slipped his hand into his trouser pocket and pulled out a small wooden box.

'Oh, for heaven's sake. I suppose you had that especially made for me too,' she said.

'Yes.'

He was the best liar she knew. And she'd been surrounded by courtiers and politicians since birth.

'What?' He looked anything but innocent. He was inviting her to enjoy the joke, but she couldn't.

She turned away.

'I'm putting it on your mantelpiece so you can think about it.'

'I've thought about it.' She'd thought of little else all

day. 'I've decided I'd rather pursue a different kind of life. I'm going to take half a dozen lovers, one for every day of the week, and I'll rest on Sundays,' she continued. 'I'm going to throw debauched parties and seduce the unwary. I'll use you as my role model.'

'You don't want to do that.'

'Oh, but I do. Purity is a construct of my own inhibitions. It's time to let those inhibitions go.'

He smiled tightly. 'As much as I agree that you should definitely explore your sensual side, I'm not a fan of your proposed method of doing so. May I suggest choosing one person to take you on that journey? More specifically, me. We could aim for one new sensory experience a day. I could teach you everything I know. Assuming you enjoy our kiss and agree to marry me.'

'I've yet to agree to kiss you at all, let alone all the rest. What if I enjoy the kiss and refuse to marry you? What if I ask you to teach me everything you know regardless? Would you do it?'

'No.'

'Why not?'

'Yawn.' He stared into his drink and then drained it in one long swallow before setting the delicately cut crystal tumbler on the mantel next to the ring box. 'It's not what I want and it's definitely not what I need. I meant what I said about commitment. I'm prepared to pay close attention to your wants and needs and see that they're met.'

She wanted to believe him, even if she couldn't quite bring herself to. 'And you expect the same from me.'

'Face it, Moriana, you've spent a lifetime making sure other people's needs are met. It's ingrained in you.'

He made her sound like a particularly comfortable leather chair. 'That's about to change. I'm on a *Moriana First* kick.'

'It's about time.' He smiled faintly. 'I happen to believe a person can be both kind to themselves and committed to the people they care about. But first things first. What is it you think I can't give you?'

Where did she begin? 'You've never been exclusive with a woman before.' Understatement.

'I've never asked one to marry me either, yet here I am.' He met her gaze, and there it was again, something hard and implacable and patient in his eyes. 'I happen to think we'd make a good team. There's fire between us; there always has been. We rub each other the wrong way. We could also rub each other the right way—so much so that there'd be no room for other lovers. That's what I believe. I'm attracted to you. I may have missed that point in the form letter.'

'You did.'

'I'm making it now.'

He was. 'Theo, you're attracted to a lot of people. You've proven that quite spectacularly over the years. Kissing me and enjoying it would prove nothing.'

'You're wrong. A kiss could prove extremely informative for us both.' He smiled that charming smile. 'Come on, Moriana. You have nothing to lose and only experience to gain. Don't you want experience?'

'Yes, but I'd rather have it without strings.'

'No strings.' She'd never seen him so obliging.

'There's an engagement ring on my mantelpiece,' she said drily.

'That's a measure of my sincerity, not a string.'

'We get this wrong, you go away,' she said firmly.

'You have my word.'

It sounded so deliciously reasonable. He was offering up his warm, willing and very attractive body for experimentation and, for all her fine talk of acquiring a legion of lovers, she didn't have the faintest idea how to actually go about getting even *one* lover in place. Men did not approach her. They never had and she had no idea if they ever would. One kiss. She could probably learn something. 'So...how do you want to do this? The kissing.'

'You tell me. However makes you comfortable.'

He was laughing at her; the little crinkle at the corner of his eyes gave it away.

'Maybe if you sat.' She waved her hand at a number of sofa and armchair options.

He unbuttoned his jacket—nothing a gentleman wouldn't do before being seated. And then he made an utter production of taking it off completely and draping it over the back of a chair. He made an even bigger production of rolling up his sleeves, his blunt nails and long fingers making deft work of it. His royal signet ring stayed on and so did his watch. He'd probably been a stripper in a former life.

'Well?' he said when he'd settled in the middle of a crimson sofa, legs wide and eyes hooded. 'What next?'

'You said I could touch you as well as kiss you.' She didn't stammer, but it was close.

'You can.'

'Right. Good. So.' She didn't move. Instead she sipped at her drink for courage, only she sipped a little too deeply and almost choked on the fire in her throat.

To his credit, he let her flounder for a full minute before breaking the silence. 'Put the drink down and come closer. It's hard to touch and kiss someone from such a distance.'

Distance. Yes. Was she really going to do this?

'What do you have to lose?' he murmured, and the answer was nothing.

Absolutely nothing.

She set her drink next to his little ring box and his empty glass and turned her back on them. She crossed to the sofa he'd claimed as his own and sank to her knees between his wide open legs, pleased when his breath faltered and his lashes fluttered closed. Was he nervous? Why would he be nervous? He wasn't the virgin here and, frankly, she was nervous enough for both of them.

She didn't even know where to look. At his shoes? The subtle sheen of his very expensive suit? His legs to either side of her? Anywhere but the not so subtle bulge in his pants. Then there was the not so small matter of where to put her hands. On his shoulders? His waist? Where? He looked altogether unsettled. 'Is this okay?'

He ran a hand over his face. 'Yes. Continue.'

Yes. Continue. Let's just seduce the playboy king with her untried self because *of course* he'd find her tentative floundering attractive. 'I don't—'

'Touch me.'

'Where?'

'Anywhere.'

'I thought you were supposed to be patient.'

'I am patient. I have the patience of a *saint*.'

'Hardly.' She put her hand on his leg, just above the knee, and felt his muscles shift. Even through the fine fabric of his suit she could feel the warmth of him. Cautiously, she circled her thumb over the inseam and slid her hand an inch or so up his leg. She'd never been this close to a man before. She'd never been invited to touch and explore.

He felt good.

She placed her other hand above his other knee and braced herself as she leaned forward, stopping just before her lips hit the juncture between skin and the snowy white collar of his shirt. She closed her eyes and let her other senses take hold. 'You smell good,' she murmured. 'What is it?'

'Soap,' he rasped, his hands now clawing at the velvet upholstery before he deliberately let out a ragged breath, tilted his head back and closed his eyes.

She drew away slightly to study his face, the frown between his eyes and rigid cord of his neck. 'Did you close your eyes so you can pretend I'm someone else?'

He opened his eyes specifically to glare at her. 'I swear on my mother's grave, Moriana, you're the most infuriating woman I know. I'm thinking of you. Get used to it.'

She could get very used to it. She moved her hands up his thighs until her fingers brushed the crease where hips met legs, her eyes widening as he gave a tiny rolling grind of his hips in response. 'You seem very...ah... responsive.'

'Yes.' A harsh rumble of a word, nothing more.

'Are you always like this?'

He had no answer for her.

She rolled her fingers, he rolled his hips, and that proved a powerful incentive to become even bolder in her exploration. It hadn't escaped her notice that Theo's eyes being closed allowed her to look wherever she wanted to look without being caught. He'd never know. And if he didn't know, how could he possibly reproach her for it?

She looked to his crotch, fascinated by the size and shape of him beneath the fine cloth. She flexed her fingers and dug into firm flesh, just a little, just below where she truly ached to touch, and he sucked in a breath but kept his eyes closed.

'Touch wherever you want,' he whispered harshly. 'I'm not going to judge.'

She traced her hands over his hips to his waist, up and over his powerful chest and the lines of his neck, she looked her fill until she reached his lips. He was biting his lower one and she didn't want that, so she touched her fingers to the spot and smoothed out the crush. His chest heaved and a broken sound escaped his lips as he turned his face towards her touch, eyes still closed, and he was beautiful in his abandon.

Was this sex? This utter acquiescence to someone else's touch?

She cradled his jaw and felt the prickles from invisible whiskers against her palm. She dragged her thumb across the seam of his lips, inordinately pleased when he parted them for her. She wanted to kiss him and keep touching him in equal measure and didn't know if she had the co-ordination for both.

She started with her lips to the underside of his jaw, close to his ear. It seemed safer than starting with a kiss to his lips and if she dragged her lips across his skin it would hardly count as a kiss at all, merely a warm-up.

'That wasn't a kiss,' she murmured against his skin. 'I'm working my way up to your lips.'

His tongue against her thumb was her only reply so she kept right on exploring, opening her own mouth and employing her tongue to learn the taste of his skin and find the pulse point in his neck, there, right there, fast and strong, and she sucked, just a little, and he groaned and the world burned that little bit hotter because of it.

She went up and over the cleft of his jaw, emboldened, but that wasn't her only area of exploration. She was working on two fronts here as she traced the long, thick length of his erection with unsteady, barely-there fingers.

She let her fingertips dance lightly over the crown and finally, finally pressed her lips against his.

One kiss, just one, because this was Theo and she believed him when he said he wouldn't judge her, and that if she didn't like it he would leave. She felt strangely safe with him.

She wanted to make the most of the opportunity he was offering.

His lips were warm and softer than she would have believed possible. He didn't invade; he let her take her time and adjust the pressure to her liking before moving forward. The tiniest tilt of her head allowed for a better fit overall. The lessening of pressure allowed her to tentatively touch her tongue to his upper lip, and the taste, oh, it was deep and dark and hinted of Scotch and flavours she wanted more of. Further exploration with her tongue was followed by the shifting of his body beneath her hand so that she cupped him more firmly, and maybe she was supposed to stroke and kiss and breathe all at once, and she probably could if the heat coursing through her body wasn't quite so overwhelming.

His tongue had come to play with hers, softly teasing, and she couldn't help her whimper or the way she wordlessly begged him to teach her more.

The sweetly subtle grind of his erection into her hand became a demanding roll.

He had no problem whatsoever co-ordinating mouth and body in a clear attempt to drive her out of her mind with lust.

It was one kiss and it blew her mind, and she couldn't breathe and she couldn't stop.

Even as he pulled his lips away from hers she ached for more.

'Breathe,' he whispered and she did, and then dropped

her head to his shoulder to hide the fact that she was already utterly undone.

'Right,' she murmured, more to herself than anyone else. 'One kiss. All done.'

She looked down and there was her hand, still laying claim to his privates. She snatched it away and he huffed out a laugh.

'Right,' he murmured.

'You said I could touch.'

'And I'd never deny it. Pour me another drink before I forget my promise *not* to touch you back.'

She pushed off him and up as gracefully as circumstances would allow. She turned her back and closed her eyes, trying not to imagine exactly how good sitting in his lap and rubbing against him might feel.

She cleared her throat. She poured the Scotch and by the time she turned back around he was standing in front of the fireplace again, his features an impassive mask.

'Did you enjoy the kiss?' he asked.

'Yes.'

'Did you enjoy putting your hands on me?'

She nodded. 'It was extremely educational, thank you.'

He took the drink from her outstretched hand. 'Are you wet for me?'

She sipped her own drink and dropped her gaze. 'Yes.'

'Marry me,' he said next.

Theo watched as Moriana crossed her hands around her tiny waist and turned away from him. Her back was ramrod-straight and her bearing regal. All those dancing or fencing lessons or whatever they were had clearly paid off. She looked at the ring box for a very long time but made no move to touch it. And then she turned back to face him.

He honestly thought she'd say yes. Between persuasive argument, the strength of that kiss and the benefits to both Arun and Liesendaach, he thought he had her.

And then she spoke.

'I'm flattered by your offer.'

It wasn't a yes.

'I'm surprised by your chivalry and more than a little stunned by my response to your...your *that*, although maybe I shouldn't be,' she continued quietly. 'You're clearly very experienced and I'm a dry river bed that's never seen rain. I would soak up as much of *that* as you'd give me. And then you'd grow bored and move on.' She shook her head, her gaze steady and shuttered. 'That wouldn't end well for either of us.'

'Why would I grow bored and move on?'

'You always do.'

'Doesn't mean I always will.'

'And then there's your family history to consider. Your marital role models, so to speak.'

Theo scowled. His parents' marriage had been... complicated. The joint state funerals for his mother, brother and father had been even more complicated. Seven of his father's mistresses had turned up for the show. Three of them had offered to comfort a fifteen-year-old Theo before the night was through. 'My parents are long dead,' he said flatly. 'Let them rest. Leave them out of this.'

'No. Your father wasn't exactly one for marital fidelity. I need to know if you want the same kind of marital relationship for us that your parents had.'

'I am not my father.'

'Nor am I your mother. She was a tolerant, pragmatic

woman who was willing to turn a blind eye to your father's many dalliances in exchange for a title and a great deal of power. I already have titles and enough power to satisfy me and I'm no longer feeling either tolerant or pragmatic. Do you really want to marry a woman who'd rather cut out her husband's eyes than have him look elsewhere for sexual pleasure?'

Bloodthirsty. He liked it. 'I'd rather keep my sight.'

'Pick a different wife and you can keep your mistresses *and* your sight.'

'Or I could be faithful to you. I don't do love, Moriana. You know it and I know it, but if you help me out in this…if you wear my ring I *will* be faithful to you. Think of it as part of our negotiation. You need it and I'm willing to accommodate it in return for your service. This isn't an area of potential conflict. Move on. Say yes.'

But she didn't say yes.

'What now?' he grated. He didn't have time for this.

'That kiss we shared, was it normal?' she asked tentatively.

He didn't know what she meant.

She sent him a look, half-pleading, half-troubled. 'I don't have the experience to know if it was good, bad or mediocre. You do.'

'It was good.' Blindingly good. 'Surely you've kissed Casimir before?'

'Not like that.' She looked away.

'Someone else?'

She shook her head.

'*Anyone* else?'

'No.'

'It was good.' Never had he cursed a woman's inexperience as much as he did in that moment. Her eyes widened as he stalked towards her. 'What would you have me do to convince you? Another kiss, perhaps? A better one?'

She didn't say no.

He wasn't patient with her the way he was before. He didn't bury his desire to touch and to take. Instead he wrapped one hand around her neck, wrapped his other arm around her waist and hauled her against him.

Her sudden rigidity shouldn't have thrilled him the way it did. Her gasp as he plundered her lips shouldn't have made him stake his claim the way he did. She opened for him, melted against him and let him own the kiss in the same way he wanted to own her.

At the age of ten, the betrothal arrangement between Moriana, Princess of Arun, and Casimir, then Crown Prince of Byzenmaach, had been nothing but an amusement to tease them with.

At fourteen, their arrangement had been like a thorn in Theo's paw. He'd known what the stirring in his trousers meant by then. Known full well he wanted her with an intensity that never waned, no matter what he did. *Pick at her, scowl at her, argue with her and, by all that was holy, don't touch her.* That had been his motto for more years than he could count.

At fifteen, his father had seen where Theo's gaze had led and told him in no uncertain terms that Moriana of Arun was off-limits. Liesendaach needed to maintain cordial relationships with bordering kingdoms far more than Theo needed to seduce a pretty princess.

At fifteen, he'd done his father's bidding.

At fifteen, his parents and brother had died and ripped Theo's heart straight out of his chest. There'd been no room for love after that. When he chased women, he'd been chasing only one thing: sweet oblivion. They'd meant nothing to him.

Standing here at thirty, he still chased sweet oblivion. The open, loving part of him had broken long ago, and no one had ever come close to fixing it—least of all him. But he could give the woman in his arms some of the things she wanted. Good things. A good life. All she had to do was let him.

He heard a groan and realised belatedly that it had come from him, but she answered with another and that was all he needed to keep going. She tasted of warm spirits and untrained passion and it shouldn't have lit a fire in him the way it did. The slide of their lips and the tangle of tongues turned to outward stillness as she learned his taste and he learned hers.

She was slender to the touch, long-legged and gently curved, and he pressed her into his hardness because to do otherwise would be sacrilege. She had both hands on his chest and he wanted her to do more. He could teach her everything she wanted to know about passion.

But not until he got what he wanted.

Theo eased out of the kiss and took his sweet time letting her go, making sure his hand stayed on her waist in case she needed steadying. She wasn't the one with a clearly visible erection but she did have a fine flush running from cheek to chest, her lips looked plump and crushed and her eyes were satisfyingly glazed.

She looked…awakened. It was an extremely good look on her.

'Our bed would not be a cold one, Princess.' Theo stepped back and reached for his jacket. 'The weight of the crown is heavy enough without adding infidelity and a spurned queen to the mix. I would not look elsewhere if I had you. We *are* sexually compatible. Save yourself the trouble of years of casual sex and take my word for it.' He let his gaze drift from her face to glance at the little wooden box on the mantelpiece. 'You know what I want.' Time to leave her be before he opted for plan C—which was to take her back into his arms and have her pregnant by morning. 'Think about it.'

CHAPTER FOUR

MORIANA SLEPT BADLY. Maybe it was because Theo's words and his kisses were on a replay loop in her brain. Maybe it was because Theo's marriage proposal was still on the table and his ring box was still unopened on her mantelpiece. Maybe it was because she was so sexually frustrated that nothing was going to fix the ache in her tonight. Whatever the reason, sleep proved elusive and there was no other option but to get out of bed, fix a post-midnight snack of banana, blueberries and unsweetened yoghurt and take it through to her sitting room. The same sitting room she'd entertained Theo in.

The room with the ring in it.

If he had commissioned the ring especially for her—and she didn't believe that for a minute, but if he had—what would he choose? Something traditional like a solitaire diamond? Something ostentatious like a coloured stone surrounded by diamonds and big enough to picnic on? Something square-cut and colourless? She wouldn't put it past him.

And there was the box, sitting oh-so-innocently on the mantel, just waiting for her to open it and find out.

She retrieved it from the ledge and set it on the side table beside her chair. There it sat until she'd finished her snack and then she picked up the box and ran her fingers across its seam. The box was beautiful in its own right—a walnut burl, polished to a dull sheen, with a maker's mark she didn't recognise. A clover leaf or some such. Pretty.

Theo of Liesendaach had offered for her, and it wasn't a joke. He'd promised to be faithful to her. He'd offered kisses that made her melt.

He'd even made her forget the debacle with Casimir and the morning's Ice Princess headlines.

Words of love had been noticeably missing from his offer—at least he'd been honest about that—but he had done something good for her this evening. He'd made her feel wanted.

Oh, she still resented his form letter proposal. She still thought marriage to him would be a volatile, love-less endeavour, but there would be benefits she hadn't previously considered.

Like him. Naked and willing.

Taking a deep breath, she closed her eyes and opened the ring box. On the count of three she opened her eyes and looked.

He'd chosen an oval, brilliant cut diamond, flanked on either side by a triangular cluster of tiny dove-grey pearls. The stones were set in a white-gold filigree almost too delicate to be believed. She'd seen some beautiful diamonds in her time, and this one was flaw-less. Not too big and unwieldy for her finger, not too small as to be overlooked. The grey pearls reminded her of her homeland, and as for the whimsical, playful design…that element put her in mind of Liesendaach. She slipped it on.

It fitted.

'Bastard,' she murmured with half-fond exasperation,

because it really did seem as if he'd chosen it with her in mind. And then her smile faded as anxiety crept back in.

How—in the space of two kisses—had he managed to make her feel so alive? He'd been so responsive, so free with his body and secure in his sexuality, so *open*. No one had ever given themselves over to her so freely and it had been better than any aphrodisiac.

He'd said it was good and she'd believed him.

There were reasons for this marriage that she could understand. A political merger, yes. Stabilisation for a region. A smart, politically aware queen could lighten her husband's load considerably. It didn't matter how hard Moriana had worked to get there, she *was* a smart and politically aware player these days. An asset to any monarch. She knew this.

She'd been worried about Theo's sexual experience and her lack of it but, after that kiss and Theo's parting words, she wasn't nearly as worried as she had been. Call it attraction, pheromones or alchemy, their kisses had been explosive.

Moriana knew she had self-esteem issues. Her utter fear of never measuring up had turned her from a curious child with a too-hot temper into a humourless, duty-bound over-thinker with an unhealthy attention to detail. A woman who thought of failure first and for whom success had always been hard won.

And then there had been Theo, telling her to touch him and that he wasn't going to judge her curiosity or her inexperience and find her wanting, and hadn't *that* been a revelation. Touching him, wanting him, enjoying him—everything had been so *effortless*.

She smirked, and then snorted inelegantly as she pictured her mother at the dining table, damning Moriana with faint praise for whatever task her daughter had tried and failed to do that day. Disguising her disappointment behind impeccable manners as she told Moriana yet again that one day she would find her true calling, something she would be instinctively good at.

Not fencing or dancing or music or drawing. Not horse riding or shooting or politics or fundraising or running a castle or making a social function an event to be remembered. She'd never been good at any of those to begin with.

But kissing Theo, she'd been good at that.

Moriana ran her hand across the sofa cushion, smoothing the velvet first one way and then digging her nails in to rough it up on the back stroke.

He'd been sitting right where she sat now, taking up more space than any one man had a right to, and she closed her eyes and wondered if she could still scent his arousal in the air. Maybe not. Maybe it was long gone.

Maybe he was right this minute taking care of his needs somewhere in the palace, and he'd damn well better be alone, his legs spread wide and his hand pressing down, just as hers was snaking down towards her panties, pushing aside the layers of silk and cotton, dipping into warmth. Maybe he had no shame whatsoever when it came to pleasing himself while remembering every shudder and every breath he'd given to her this evening.

Why *should* there be shame in this?

Her fingers moved quickly and her body grew taut. She'd always known what her body could do in this regard, how lost she could get. She'd never before thought of her inherent sensuality as a strength, but Theo had it too and tonight he'd shown her how he wielded his, succumbed to it, even as he owned it, until it was more than just a strength.

It was a gift.

* * *

The headlines the following morning were still not kind to Princess Moriana of Arun. She'd found the newspapers in their usual place in the breakfast room and had mistakenly thought that their presence heralded other more appealing news than her love life or lack of it.

Not so.

Out of Her League one paper proclaimed, with a picture of her and Theo from last night beneath the headline. The photographer had caught them as they'd been discussing the merits of the Vermeer. Theo looked sharp-eyed and handsome, the edges of his lips tilted towards a smile but not quite getting there as he studied the painting. She'd been looking at Theo and the photographer had captured her from behind. There was something vulnerable about the lines of her shoulders and neck and the curve of her cheek. From the position of their bodies, it was obvious her attention had been on Theo rather than the painting. Her hand had been resting on his sleeve, and instead of it looking like a courtesy on his part it looked like a desperate plea for attention on hers.

Great. Just great. She tossed the paper aside and picked up the next one.

The Fall and Fall of Arun's Perfect Princess this one said, and the photo must have been taken when she first saw Theo and her brother stepping into the auction room last night because she looked gutted. It was there in her eyes, in the twist of her lips. One single moment of despair at her brother's betrayal and they'd caught it; of course they had. Her mother would have been horrified by such a vulgar display of emotion. Moriana didn't much care for it herself. Not in public. Masks should never slip in public. All that ever did was invite predators to circle.

The article went on to criticise her dress, her shoes and her too-slender frame, and suggest she needed professional help in order to cope with her rejection. Arun's relationship with Byzenmaach was now strained, they said. Trust between the two kingdoms had been shattered and she *knew* that wasn't true, only there it was in black and white.

And then Theo walked into the breakfast room and drew her attention away from the hateful words.

He wore his customary dark grey trousers and white dress shirt but he'd done away with the tie and undone the first two buttons on his shirt.

'You're still here,' she said, and he nodded agreeably.

'I still need a wife.'

Half-dressed and unashamedly comfortable in his skin, he leaned over her shoulder and plucked a paper from the pile she'd already looked at before settling into the chair next to hers to read it.

'*Two-timing Princess,*' he read aloud. 'Go you.'

'Read on,' she muttered. '*You're* a ruthless despoiler of all that is pure and good in this world.'

'Of course I am. How is this even news?' He put that paper down and picked up another and was smirking two minutes later. 'Don't let anyone ever tell you those shoes you wore last night were a bad fashion choice. The shoes were good.'

The shoes had been vintage Jimmy Choo. Damn right they were good. 'You're reading the one about how I was dressed for seduction last night in a desperate attempt to end civilisation as we know it and finally get lucky?'

'I am. You should dress for boar-hunting one evening. Knee-high leather boots, armguards, stiffened leather corset, breeches and a forest-green coat that sweeps the floor and hides your weapons. See what they make of that.'

He was even better than Aury at mocking press articles. He truly didn't seem to give a damn what was printed about them.

'Doesn't it bother you? All these stories?'

'No.' His voice turned hard and implacable. 'And it shouldn't bother you. The only reason the press are on you now is because you've never been at the centre of any scandal before and they're hungry for more. Strangely enough, now is the perfect time to reinvent yourself in the eyes of your public—assuming that's something you want to do. Or you could mock them. Tell them you're pregnant with triplets and don't know who the father is. Make Casimir's day. *Four* royal bastards for the new King of Byzenmaach.'

'Oh, you cruel man.'

'Made you smile though, didn't it?'

She couldn't deny it.

Finally he turned his attention away from the newspapers. She could pinpoint the moment he truly looked at her, because her body lit up like sunrise.

'Good morning,' he murmured. 'Nice dress.'

She'd worn one of her favourite casual dresses from the same section of her wardrobe where the red gown usually hung. It was part of her 'love it but where can I wear it?' collection. It was lemon yellow, strapless, snug around the bodice and flared gently from the waist to finish a couple of inches above her knees. She'd kept her jewellery modest. Two rings for her fingers—neither of them *his* ring—a pair of diamond studs for her ears, and that was it. Her sandals were the easy on and off kind and she'd caught her hair back in a messy ponytail that spoke of lazy weekend sleep-ins.

'Yeah, well. Maybe I'm out to seduce you.'

'A for Effort,' he murmured. 'That dress is a weapon. You need to be photographed in it looking all tumbled and content. With me.' He picked up the pile of still unread papers and dumped them on the ground between their two chairs.

'I hadn't finished with those yet.'

'They were making you unhappy. Why read them?' He reached for a croissant and the blackberry jam. 'I need you to be more resilient in the face of bad press. I honestly thought you were.'

She wasn't. Not at all. 'And it bothers you that I'm not?'

'It bothers me a lot.' For the first time this morning he sounded deadly serious. 'Liesendaach's court can be hard to navigate. My uncle's legacy of corruption still lingers, and every time I think I've stamped it out, it comes back. I don't trust my politicians or my advisors. I barely trust my palace staff. You *will* get bad press if you marry me. You *will* get people trying to befriend you and use you in the hope that you can influence me on their behalf. I can't protect you from either of those things, so I need to know in advance that they won't break you. I need you to know that some days it's going to feel as if the world is out to get you and no one has your back.'

'You're not exactly selling your marriage proposal this morning, are you?'

'Not yet. I'm mainly mentioning the fine print. But I will be selling it. Soon.' He shot her a quick glance. 'Just as soon as I think you're up for an onslaught.'

'Maybe after my next cup of coffee,' she murmured.

He reached for the coffee pot and offered to top her up but she shook her head so he filled his own cup. 'How did you sleep?'

'Poorly. Your ring is lovely, by the way. I lasted until almost two a.m. before looking at it.'

'Well done.' He smiled wryly. 'I notice you don't have it on.'

'Don't push. I'm considering your proposal. Yesterday, I wasn't even doing that.'

'Yesterday, you thought me indifferent to you. Now you know I'm not.'

'Which means you now get a hearing. It doesn't mean we're ready for marriage. Why the rush?'

'Well, we could always wait for old age.' He was annoyed and doing little to hide it.

'There's something you're not telling me.' She'd been around him long enough to know that this relentless pushing wasn't usually his style. 'You're too urgent. You're pushing too hard for this to happen and making mistakes in your approach. It's not like you.'

A muscle flickered in his jaw.

Something was very definitely up. 'Spill,' she murmured. 'I know you're under pressure to marry. Liesendaach wants a queen and you need an heir. But I didn't think you were under this much pressure.'

'My uncle is petitioning for my dismissal,' Theo said finally. 'He can't get me on fiscal incompetence or general negligence. I do my job and I do it well. But there's a loophole that allows a monarch of Liesendaach to be replaced if they haven't married and produced an heir by the time they turn thirty. We didn't even know it was there until my uncle found it and raised it. I turned thirty last month. I can challenge the clause at a judicial level, no problem. Buy myself some time. But the best way to address the petition is for me to secure a fiancée and schedule a wedding as soon as possible. When Casimir let you down I saw a solution I could live with. Meaning you.'

'And here I was beginning to think you had a crush on me all these years and simply couldn't wait to claim me now that I was free.'

'That too. I should have led with that.'

'I wouldn't have believed you.' Moriana definitely needed more coffee this morning.

Theo sighed and started slathering jam on his croissant. 'There's no talking to you this morning, is there?'

'Not before the caffeine hits my bloodstream. So who will you marry if you don't marry me? A Cordova twin?' The Cordova twins had made a splash last year, when they'd taken turns dating him. One twin one week, the other twin the next. It had gone on for months. Theo either hadn't cared or hadn't noticed.

'You're picking a fight that's not there.'

'And here I thought I was identifying an alternative solution to your problem.'

His eyes flashed silver and his lips thinned. 'You're a better one.'

'I know.' There was no point pretending the Cordova women were better options when it came to political connections. 'But you have to look at your offer from my point of view too. For the first time in my life I'm free to do what I please. I want to cut loose and have some fun. I want some romance.' She gave a helpless little shrug. 'I know what your offer means. I know the work involved. There's a lifetime of it, and I'm not sure it's what I want.'

'Yet you were all set to marry Casimir.' His voice had cooled. 'You wanted it once.'

She had. She'd looked forward to it. So what made Theo's offer so disturbingly different?

Breakfast continued in silence until finally she could stand the silence no more. 'I spoke to Casimir this morning.'

Theo looked up from his breakfast but made no comment.

'I'm investigating my flaws. I had ten years in which to kiss him properly and I didn't. Nor did he ever push for more. We spoke about that.'

Theo raised his eyebrow. 'Did he tell you he was celibate? Blind? Hormonally challenged?'

'No, but thank you for the suggestions for my own utter apathy.'

'You weren't apathetic last night.'

Maybe that was what was different about this offer of marriage. Casimir had never really hurt her with his indifference because Moriana had been similarly indifferent right back. But Theo—she wasn't indifferent to him, and never had been. He could wind her up at whim and leave her reeling, without any effort whatsoever. And that was a dangerous position for a queen to be in.

'Casimir mentioned that—for him—chemistry with another person starts well before the kissing,' she began hesitantly. 'He said there's an awareness between two people, a connection that can't be faked. He said that good kisses, spectacular kisses, were as much about letting someone into your head as they were a physical thing. He said kissing random strangers and expecting to see fireworks was a stupid idea.'

'Remind me to send him a fruit basket,' said Theo.

'I told him you'd offered for me. He laughed.'

'A fruit basket minus the strawberries.'

'Why did he laugh?'

'I'm not a mind-reader, Moriana. You'd have to ask him.'

She had.

Casimir had mumbled something about everything falling into place. He'd wished her every happiness, told her she'd be happier with Theo than she ever would have been with him, and she'd cut the call shortly thereafter. It was that or start wailing at her former intended for being an arrogant moron.

'He did give me one nice compliment,' she offered wryly. 'He's going to miss our political conversations. He said I have great depth of knowledge and an impressive ability to influence decisions. His and beyond. I'm a political muse. Go me.'

Theo's gaze grew carefully shuttered. 'The unseen hand.'

'A guiding hand,' she corrected.

'I don't need one.'

'You've never had one.' But she was one, with intimate knowledge of how deals were done across four kingdoms.

Theo said nothing.

'You offer physical intimacy with such a sure hand,' she murmured. 'But would you ever seek my counsel?'

'I'd…think about it,' he said with a twist of his lips that suggested discomfort. 'I find it difficult to trust people. Anyone.'

'And you would include me with the masses? Don't you want to be able to trust your wife?'

'When it comes to trusting people, it's not really about what I want. It's about what I'm prepared to lose.'

'Wow. You really are alone. In your head and in your heart.' She couldn't quite comprehend how a king who trusted no one could function in office. 'Aren't you lonely?'

'No.'

'So *the main duty* of a queen towards her king—that of offering full and frank emotional, political, social and *well-being* support to the man behind the throne—you don't want it.'

He said nothing.

Moriana sat back in her chair, still stunned. 'Seriously, Theo, you don't need me. Just pick anyone.'

He didn't like that, she could tell. But she didn't much care for the position he was offering either.

'I mean it,' she said. 'I am not trained to sit at your side and do nothing. I need your trust in order to function as your queen. Without it, I'm worse than useless. And I will *not* be rendered useless this time around.'

'Come to Liesendaach for the week,' he offered abruptly. 'And I'll try and give you what you want.'

'Not want. Need. This one's a deal-breaker,' she finished quietly.

'Trust takes time,' he snapped, and, yes, she'd give him that.

'I have time. You might not, but if you want my co-operation I suggest you make time. I can deal with a marriage minus the love. I've been prepared for that for a long time. But I'm telling you plain, I will not become your queen until I have your absolute trust.'

'Is that your final position?'

She nodded.

'Then I'll try. There can be political discussion and getting to know each other and a great deal of kissing and touching and fun. You might like it more than you think.'

'Perhaps. Okay, here's the deal. I *need* your trust. But I *want* more sexual expertise. I'd like to prioritise both, this coming week in Liesendaach. Can we do that?'

It was as if her question flipped a switch in him. His uncertainty bled away, leaving a confident, sharp-eyed negotiator in its wake. 'I'll do you a deal,' he murmured.

She stopped ripping her pastry into ever smaller pieces and brushed her fingers against each other to rid them of crumbs before reaching for her napkin and squeezing. 'I'm listening.'

'I'm prepared to offer you a minimum of one new sexual experience each and every day of your stay,' he continued. 'As an offer of good faith I'll even throw in a lesson here and now at the breakfast table. But if at any time during our lessons you climax for me...from that point onwards you wear my ring.'

'No deal.' She didn't trust her body to remain sufficiently restrained during these lessons. He'd have her seeing stars so fast she'd be wearing his ring by lunchtime.

'Okay, I'll do you a new deal. What if you were able to stop me with a word at any point during a lesson? Climax averted, so to speak. Everyone backs off to allow for breathing space. We could even think of it as an exercise in trust-building. No commitment or ring-wearing required. Easy.'

'It doesn't sound that easy.'

His eyes gleamed. 'Some lessons *are* harder than others. You did say you wanted to learn. Also, it'll be fun. You said you wanted that too. I'm merely attempting to provide some for you.'

'Good of you.'

'I know.'

The room temperature jacked up a notch as their gazes clashed and she contemplated just how badly wrong this week could go. 'You're offering me a week full of fun, sex education, political discourse and trust-building exercises? What about romance?' She'd bet he wouldn't offer that.

'The offer includes romance. You'd be a fool not to see if I can deliver.'

Even if he didn't deliver, she'd quite like to see him *try*.

And they said she didn't have a sense of humour.

'Agreed,' she murmured. 'Let's go to Liesendaach for a week.'

He sat back, pushed his meal aside. 'First lesson starts now. You might want to lock the doors.'

Even as she dropped her napkin across her plate and headed for the double doors that would take her from the room, Moriana still didn't know whether she would lock the doors or not.

Theo was playing her, she knew that much.

But maybe, just maybe, she wanted to be played with.

She closed the doors and locked them, and then did the same to the doors on the other side of the room. She stood there, with her eyes closed and her back to him for a moment, trying to find her equilibrium but it was gone.

He thought her innocent, and in a physical sense she was. She'd never been touched, she'd never had sex. But she was twenty-eight years old and there was no cap on her imagination. In her imagination, she'd had any number of sexual experiences. She knew exactly what kind of things he might teach her. She could describe them in great detail.

And, oh, how she wanted to see if the reality lived up to her imagination.

'Come here.' Even his voice could seduce her when he wanted it to.

She took a deep breath, opened her eyes and turned. He was right where she'd left him. She walked towards him, feigning a confidence she didn't have.

He smiled.

He'd pushed away from the table and sat sprawled in his chair and he indicated the cleared space where his meal had once been. 'Sit on the table.'

He could have her for breakfast.

She half leant, half sat, hands curling around the table edge, and all the time he watched her like a hawk. She could feel the weight of his gaze and the assessment behind it as he sized her up and planned his approach.

'Your dress has a zip at the back. Undo it.' The purr was back in his voice and so was the edge of command.

'Why should I?' She was embarrassed to undress for him here in broad daylight. It smacked of her owning her actions when maybe, just maybe, she wanted to be led. 'You have hands.' They were very nice hands. Large and strong-looking, with short nails and an appealing ruggedness about them.

'And I'll use them. Right now I'm more interested in watching you undress for me. You blush so beautifully.'

Well, he would know. He could make her blush with a glance, and if that didn't work all he had to do was use his words. Haltingly, she fumbled behind her back and slid the zip down to her waist. The bodice of her dress had boning and would stay up unless pushed.

He raised an aristocratic eyebrow.

She pushed the top part down and folded her arms around her waist for protection. Moments later she unfolded her arms again, dropped them to her sides and curled her hands over the table edge in a desperate bid to at least *appear* a little more casually confident than she was.

She still had a bra on. It was white, strapless and covered almost as much as the dress had.

His eyes grew intent and he reached out to draw a path from her collarbone to the very top of her bra, tracking the shape of it with his fingertips as it fell away under her arms. 'This too.'

Her nipples pebbled at his words and he rewarded them by stroking his thumb gently across one of them, back and forth, back and forth, causing the tug of want in her belly to pull tight. She reached behind her for the hook and the bra fell away—he helped it fall away.

'Your breasts are perfect.' He sounded almost angry.

They were a little on the small side, as far as she was concerned, and right now they were aching for more than just the flick of his thumb, but the appropriate response to a compliment, sincere or not, had been drummed into her since birth. 'Thank you.'

Heat stole into her cheeks and across her chest and she looked away from his fierce, bright gaze. The wall was right there, suitably dressed with a painting. Nothing abnormal about that wall. The only abnormal thing in this room was her. And maybe Theo. Or maybe sitting half naked atop the breakfast table *was* normal in his world. 'What next?'

He moved, and she closed her eyes and when she felt his lips on her they weren't where she'd expected him to put them. He'd placed them just below her left ear and she shivered when his tongue came out to trace a delicate circle.

'Promises,' she muttered and she could feel his smile on her skin.

'Patience.' He placed his hands either side of hers and continued to kiss a leisurely path across to her lips, where he proceeded to tease and tempt and never give her any actual substance.

'I hate you,' she muttered next.

'You shouldn't. I'm giving you my best.'

He went lower, with his hair brushing her neck as he

kissed her collarbone and the swell of her upper breast, and *now* they were getting somewhere. Her nipples had been tightly furled since she'd unzipped her dress and now they were throbbing and desperate for attention. She pushed up against him, not begging, but hoping, and he responded by drawing that tiny circle with the tip of his tongue again and then pulling back to blow on the skin he'd just licked.

Heat pooled low in her stomach and made her gasp. Dear heaven, he was good at this.

He kissed her some more, lighting a fire beneath her skin, and then finally he closed his mouth around her nipple and sucked.

'Oh.' She kept her legs tightly closed and rode out the thrumming clench of pleasure his actions had caused.

A lick for her other breast now, and then he obliged by closing his mouth over it and suckling hard. There. That. The fierce pull of want and the heady coil of desire. She moaned her pleasure, and he grazed her with his teeth. And then his lips were on hers again only this time he was claiming her, devouring her, and she melted into that too. She went where he led, mindless and willing, and when he pulled back and studied her again with glittering grey eyes she obligingly caught up on her breathing.

'Nice,' she whispered raggedly. 'Good lesson.'

'There's more.'

She wasn't at all sure she was ready for more.

'Raise your skirt,' he ordered gruffly.

'I—' There was a whole world of imagination waiting for her in that region. 'What's the lesson?'

'The lesson is that compliance has its rewards.'

She met his darkly mocking smile with a level stare.

At least she hoped that was what her face was doing. She'd rather *not* look like a startled fawn.

'Of course, if you don't comply you'll never know,' he murmured.

He knew he had her; she could see it in his eyes. He knew exactly how badly she wanted to know. Not just to imagine her sexual encounters but to *know* what one felt like.

With as much shamelessness as she could muster, she put her hands on the skirt of her frock and slid it slowly up her thighs, up and up until he could see her underwear. She'd worn white panties today, with tiny black polka dots, and they were pretty but nothing special. Not skimpy, not lacy, just normal. She wondered whether he would ask her to take them off.

'Good.' She could barely hear his low rumble. 'Now put your hands back on the table and lean back a little.'

The skirt stayed up, her head stayed low and her hands went back on the table as she waited for his next move.

His hands finally settled either side of her thighs, the heat of his body engulfing her as he set his lips to that place where her pulse beat frantically in her neck.

'You drive me mad, Moriana. You always have. You think you're so flawed.'

His next kiss landed on her shoulder and she shuddered her surrender. The kiss after that touched the outer curve of her breast and avoided her nipple, but not for long. He left no part of her breasts and belly uncovered as he worked his way down to her panties, and by the time he got there she was a flushed and writhing mess.

'I tend to think you're rather perfect,' he murmured as his breath ghosted over her underwear. He pushed them aside a little and licked. She'd heard about this.

Hell, she'd *dreamed* of it. But not in the broad light of day, and not in the breakfast room.

Slowly, hesitantly, she slid her hand down over the front of her panties, putting a barrier between herself and him. She didn't know if she wanted him to continue his exploration or not. On the one hand, there was embarrassment. On the other hand, her fingers found the damp, swollen groove, even over her panties, and her eyes closed on an involuntary shudder.

'What are you doing?' he rasped, looking up at her with a glittering warning in his eyes.

'Helping.'

'Hands on the table, Moriana. I don't need any *help*.'

And then his hands were high on her thighs, gently parting her legs. Moments later something soft and warm and moist found her hard little nub through already moist panties, and she thought it was his finger but both his hands were well and truly accounted for, wrapped around her thighs as they were, and his hair was tickling her inner thigh and, yes, indeed, that right there was his tongue.

It was even more spectacular than she'd imagined.

Heat flooded through her and she didn't know whether to scramble away or stay right where she was. There was another option, of course, and that was to give him as much room as possible so he could keep right on doing what he was doing.

Option three won.

'Hold on,' he muttered, and then he was pushing her legs wide apart and her panties aside and then his mouth was on her, kissing and kissing and flicking and sucking and *kissing*. It was too much. It was not enough. Her hand raked its way through his hair before she could even think to hold back, and *there*, right there, as she whimpered and began climbing through clouds.

Not yet.

Not. Yet.

Up and up and up.

'Stop!'

He stopped. He kept his word, his chest rising and his shoulders granite-hard as he pulled back and rested his forehead on her knee, his hands still curved high on each thigh, holding her open, keeping her in place. One more stroke was all it would take to topple her. She closed her eyes and pushed his hands away. Closed her legs and bit down on a whimper, because even the clench of her thighs had almost been enough to send her soaring.

'What do you want?'

He sounded ragged, almost as desperate as she'd been, and she laughed weakly and pressed the heel of her palm down over her centre to try and stave off completion and wasn't that a mistake. She was too close to climax.

'Oh, no...' she whimpered. 'No— Stop...stop... stop...'

He wasn't even touching her and she was toast, soaring, and cursing, and toppling over onto her side on the table as she rode out the waves breaking inside her body.

Control. She didn't have it. Another tremor racked her. 'That was—that.' She was vastly surprised she still had the power of speech. 'Phew! That was *close*.'

He barked out a laugh and she gathered her courage and continued with the deception.

'Yeah.' She pushed her cheek into the cool wooden table and tried not to drool through her smile as she cracked one eye open the better to see his response. 'Really close. You almost had me there.'

'Princess, I *got* you there. You came. I win.'

'No. I didn't come.' Lies, all lies, as another wave rode her hard. She fought the lassitude that followed in its wake by pushing up off the table and into a sitting position, hands either side of her and her legs pressed tightly together. She had a fair idea what she looked like, but she'd see to herself in a minute. She was far more interested in what Theo looked like, and he didn't disappoint. His eyes glittered fiercely and his colour was high, as if he was either mightily aroused or mightily annoyed. It was hard to say which sentiment rode him harder. His lips were moist, his jaw tight. His crotch was…well. It was reassuring to know she hadn't been the only one enjoying the lesson.

'You came.' He sounded so utterly confident.

'No, I *almost* came.' She looked for her bra and found it at the far end of the table. She wrapped it around her and fastened it quickly. The reapplication of her dress took longer, mainly because it was all askew and tangled around her waist. She figured her legs would probably hold her but she kept one hand to the table just in case, as she stood up and tried to get dressed. Panties—they were already on and damper than a wet cloth. Bra—on. Dress—

'Turn around and let me help,' he muttered.

So she turned around and he zipped her up and then smoothed her dress down over her curves. 'You came,' he murmured in her ear. 'You know it. And I'd trust you a whole lot more if you admitted it.'

Damn. She couldn't look at him. She didn't want to uphold her end of the bargain. 'I can't.'

'Hard, isn't it? Knowing when and who to trust,' he offered silkily.

She stepped away to reclaim her shoes. 'Time will tell.'

'I'll give you a pass this time because that's what you seem to need but, I promise you, your body's not that hard to read.' His words licked at her. 'You're headily responsive, Moriana, but I do know what I'm doing. This time I *wanted* you to come for me. Next time I'm going to keep you on the edge of satisfaction until you're begging for release.'

He was better at these games than she was. 'That sounds…'

'Cruel?' he asked. 'Depraved? Torturous?'

'Kind of perfect.' She smoothed back her hair and wondered how she was going to explain her current state of dishevelment to her lady-in-waiting. Maybe she could set Aury to packing for Liesendaach by way of distraction.

'So,' she began, and if she was a little throaty, a little breathless, it couldn't be helped. Having Theo's warmth at her back and his words in her ear did that to her. 'I'm coming to Liesendaach for a week, and at this point I won't be wearing your ring. Any social functions I should know about?'

He hadn't given up when it came to seducing her into marrying him. The glittering promise in his eyes told her he was just getting started. She was flustered, still reeling from the negotiating and the kissing and the not so simple act of resisting him.

The trust issues between them were a little bit heartbreaking.

'One State Dinner on Friday, four luncheons, bring riding gear if riding's something you like to do, and you're going to need at least half a dozen breakfast outfits similar to the one you have on. We'll be breakfasting together every morning. Think of it as lesson time.'

'And in the evening? What do you do of an evening?'

'Usually I work.'

'Oh.' She was ever so slightly disappointed. 'I'll bring some of my work too. You don't mind?'

'I don't mind. Or we could occasionally meet for a nightcap.'

'We could.'

He was laughing at her, not outwardly, but she could still sense his amusement. She was like putty after only one of his lessons. Totally malleable and greedy for more of his attention, never mind that he'd just given her more than she could handle.

'When would you like to leave?' Thankfully she could still manage to ask a sensible question.

'Whenever you're ready.'

Still so *amenable*. She was looking forward to this week. 'I can be ready within the hour if you'd like to leave this morning? My lady-in-waiting can follow later this afternoon with a suitable wardrobe and my work.'

'Let's do that.'

'Theo.' He was a king in need of a queen, a ruler with a genuine predicament and she respected that he was trying to solve his problem. 'I'm not going to meekly say yes to marriage after a week with you on your best behaviour. You might be wasting your time.'

'I'm not wasting my time. I know you'll give me a fair trial, and that you'll be looking at ways to make this work for you and everyone else around you. You won't be able to help yourself.' He held her gaze and she couldn't read the look in his eyes. 'It's what you do.'

CHAPTER FIVE

THE ROYAL PALACE of Liesendaach was exactly as Theo had left it. Grey slate roofs, creamy sandstone walls arranged in a U-shape around a huge central courtyard that could fit a small army. Six hundred and eighty-five white-sashed windows graced the building. The front half of the palace was surrounded by immaculately kept lawns and the back half of the palace grounds was a series of garden rooms, radiating outwards like the spokes of a wheel.

The palace employed fourteen full-time gardeners and many more seasonal workers, and every spring and autumn he opened the gardens to the public and allowed tours and special events to take place there. It was an incredible waste of water, according to some, but Theo's gardeners knew better than to be wasteful with the precious resource. They were forever experimenting with hardy plant varieties and watering regimes. The forest that bordered the gardens on three sides kept the worst of the hot drying winds away in summertime and took the edge off the icy north winds in winter. Theo's ancestors had known what they were doing when they'd kept the forest in place centuries ago. Naysayers could kiss his royal brass before he let anyone dismiss the gardens as frivolous.

They more than paid their way.

Moriana had been to the palace before, but not lately. Theo signalled to the helicopter's pilot to loop around the building to give her a bird's eye view.

The palace of her birth was starkly grey and forbidding, and beautiful in its own way. This place probably looked like a blowsy showgirl in comparison, but he wanted her to like it.

'The beauty here is not just for beauty's sake,' he said, leaning over her shoulder to look out of the window at the orchard. 'A lot of botanical research takes place here, education for schoolchildren, animal husbandry and breeding programmes, patronage of the arts—'

'Theo,' she interrupted gently. 'I know. Liesendaach's royal palace is and should always remain both functional and beautiful. You've no need to defend it. Not to me.'

'Do you have any idea how you might split your allegiance between Liesendaach and Arun?'

She turned to look him in the eye and her smile was bittersweet. 'You need to read the *Princess Handbook*,' she said. 'If I take your name my loyalty will be to Liesendaach.'

'But how would you feel about that?'

'Given the caning I'm getting in Arun's papers at the moment, I'd feel quite vengefully good about it. On a more practical note, it might just give my brother the incentive to take a wife.' She turned back to look out of the helicopter window. 'Your country has been without a queen for almost two decades. For me that means no recent shoes to step into, no impossible expectations. There's just me and what I might make of the role, and that's liberating in a way. I'm not scared.' Her lips twisted. 'I've been well trained. Byzenmaach would have given me that fresh start too.'

He didn't like the reminder of Byzenmaach and her future there up until a few days ago. A couple of kisses and a tiny taste of her and already he was feeling a possessiveness he'd never felt before. 'Byzenmaach's loss.'

'Indeed.'

They landed, both of them well used to getting in and out of helicopters. Theo had been hoping to make a quiet entrance but his Head of Household Staff had other ideas. Samantha Sterne stood waiting for them at the entrance closest to the helipad and one look at her ultra-serene demeanour promised a storm of rare intensity. The calmer she appeared, the worse the problem was.

'Sam,' he said. 'Meet Princess Moriana of Arun, my guest for the week. You got my message about readying the Queen's chambers?'

Moriana might not be wearing his ring but he could make it clear in a multitude of ways that she was no ordinary guest.

'Yes, Your Majesty.' Sam turned and curtseyed to Moriana. 'My apologies, Your Highness. The maids are finishing up now. The suite is clean but hasn't been in use for some time. I wanted it aired, fresh flowers brought in, new linens…'

'And he gave you fifteen minutes' notice?'

Sam smiled slightly at Moriana's dry words. 'Something like that, Your Highness.'

'Sam, is it?'

'Yes, Your Highness. Head of Household Staff.'

'Ma'am is fine.'

'Yes, ma'am.' Sam nodded, but didn't move on. 'Your Majesty.' She turned back towards Theo and there it was, the surface calm that spoke of a major problem. 'Your cousin arrived this morning, requesting an audience with you. When you weren't here he insisted on waiting, no matter how long it took. I put him in his old suite. George is currently seeing to his needs.'

'I'll take care of it.' Cousin Benedict had called the royal palace home during the years his father—Theo's uncle—had been Regent. He'd never shown any outward desire for the throne, preferring a playboy lifestyle to one of service, but he was a troublemaker at heart and a sly one at that. Family on the one hand; one laughing breath away from stabbing Theo in the back on the other. Benedict hadn't actively sought his company in years.

Sam nodded and took her leave, her stiletto heels clicking rapidly across the polished marble floor. Theo turned to see Moriana watch the other woman go, her expression assessing.

'She's very young to be your Head of Staff,' said Moriana finally.

'The old one was loyal to my uncle. This one's not.' That wasn't the line of thought he was expecting. His mind was still on Benedict.

'She's very pretty.'

'She's very competent.'

'I hope so. There are people I'll want to bring with me to Liesendaach if we do go ahead with a union.'

'Your Head of Household Staff?' he asked drily.

'No, Augustus would kill me. I'm merely pointing out that some staffing changes and additions will be inevitable. I like things done a certain way and I'm not shy about making it happen. Don't worry,' she murmured. 'If Samantha Sterne is as competent as she is pretty, she won't be going anywhere. What's up with Benedict?'

'You mean besides the usual? It's hard to say.'

'You were close to him for a while, weren't you?'

'If by *close* you mean that after my parents died he and I set about creating as much havoc as we could, then yes, we were close. I grew up. He grew petulant. And now would be a very good time to slip my ring on your finger if you wanted to. For your protection. Not that I'm harping on, but I don't trust my cousin not to skewer you when you're not looking. It's his specialty.'

'And how exactly is wearing your ring going to protect me from that? Because I would have thought it painted a target on my back. Unless competing with you for something you've laid claim to is something your cousin *never* does.'

He and Benedict had often made a game out of competing for women; he couldn't deny it. 'It'd still make me feel better.'

'Ownership usually does.'

Ouch.

'Ring or no ring, I can handle cousin Benedict,' she said with a smile. 'Shall we see what he wants?'

Benedict could wait. 'Let me show you to your rooms and then *I'll* see what he wants.'

'Of course, Your Majesty.'

He wasn't nervous about showing her his home. He wasn't suddenly sweating, hoping she'd like her quarters, and the artwork, and the gardens, and the people. He wasn't.

It was just warm in here.

Moriana knew Theo's palace was beautiful. She'd been there before, in its ballrooms and Theo's living quarters when he was growing up. But she'd never been in his mother's rooms before and she hadn't quite realised how stunning the incoming light from a wall full of windows would be, or how magnificent the second storey view out over the gardens would be. The floor of the Queen's chambers consisted of polished wooden parquetry in a

floral design and the ceiling was high and domed. Someone, at some point, had fallen in love with chandeliers,
and they caught the sunlight and scattered it.

'There are other suites to choose from.' Theo was
watching her, waiting for her reaction. She walked towards the windows to stare out, not wanting to drool.

'This'll do.'

'I can bring in some grey stone. Make you feel more
at home.'

She turned in a circle, feasting her eyes on absolutely
everything. 'Don't you dare.' Okay, maybe she could be
seen to drool a little bit.

And there was Theo, hands in his trouser pockets
and his back to the wall, standing just inside the door.
Watching her. 'Where are your rooms?'

'The other side of the hall, with windows facing east.
I get the sunrise, you get the sunset.'

'But do you have chandeliers?' she said.

'You want to see my rooms?'

She did.

His suite was situated on the other side of the long
hallway. There were more windows. Lots of tans and
blues, hidden lights rather than chandeliers and the pick
of the artwork. She eyed the Botticelli painting over his
decorative fireplace with frank interest and heard a faint
growl from somewhere behind her.

'You can't have it,' he murmured. 'You want to look
at it, you can come here.'

'But *would* I look at it if I came here? That's the question.' If it came to a competition as to whether she'd be
more likely to study Theo or that painting, Theo would
win. She still hadn't forgotten what he'd taught her this
morning at the breakfast table. She wondered what he

could teach her in a living room with soft surfaces all around them.

'I could be persuaded to have more than one lesson per day,' she said, eyeing the nearby sofa.

'I need to preserve my strength.' He looked darkly amused.

'Ah, well. Tomorrow morning, then.' She didn't linger during her tour of his rooms. It felt a little like trespassing, for all that he seemed to have no problem with her being there. He kept to the corners of his rooms as well, whereas she was currently standing in the middle of a parquetry circle that was itself probably the dead centre of the room. She let him escort her back to her quarters, where he obligingly made way for two chambermaids, one carrying a vase, the other with her arms full of blooming roses that left a fragrant trail in their wake, but he didn't make to follow her inside. 'I'll leave you to settle in,' he said. 'If you want anything changed or moved, call Sam.'

Moriana nodded. 'Give your cousin my regards. Will I see him at dinner?'

'On Friday at the State Dinner, yes. He's on the guest list.'

'So you do still socialise with him on occasion?'

'It's unavoidable.'

'But you won't be inviting him to stay on, now that he's here?' She couldn't fathom Theo's relationship with his cousin.

'No. He won't be staying on.'

'Because I'm here?'

'That's one of the reasons, yes.'

'Benedict has always been courteous to me,' she said.

'I'm sure he has. You are sister to a king. You were betrothed to a crown prince. You outrank him. Besides, why make enemies when you can charm someone instead?'

That was one way of looking at it. 'How come *you* never embraced that philosophy around me?'

'You were annoying.' He smiled as he said it, and for a moment she felt the heat of his laser-like focus. 'If Benedict stays, my attention will be split. I'd rather concentrate on you alone.'

'Very charming,' she murmured. And she quite enjoyed the view as she watched him go.

Theo didn't have to go looking for his cousin. Five minutes after stepping into his office, Benedict found him. Benedict was two years older than Theo, two inches shorter and as vain as any peacock. He appeared in the doorway to Theo's office, wearing a sneer Theo strongly hoped wasn't hereditary. Benedict had introduced a teenage Theo to Europe's fleshpots and vices, and back then Theo had needed no encouragement to make the most of them. Still finding his way after the death of his parents and older brother, he'd found a willing companion in Benedict.

But Benedict, for all his easy grace and charm, had a viciousness and immorality about him that couldn't be ignored. Theo had started pulling back from their exploits. Benedict hadn't liked that.

It had gone steadily downhill from there.

'You could say hello and offer me a drink,' Benedict said.

'I assumed you'd already helped yourself,' Theo replied, turning his attention momentarily from the other man to finish an email response to his secretary. 'What do you want?'

'The palace requested my presence at dinner on Friday so here I am.'

'You're early.'

'Quite. Had I known you were returning with a guest I may not have made myself quite so at home. On the other hand I get to watch you try to impress the lovely Princess of Arun. That could be fun.'

'Benedict, you specifically asked to see me and I was given to understand that you thought the matter important enough to wait for my return. What do you want?'

'A couple of things. First, the petition for you to marry and reproduce or get off the throne is being abandoned. I never supported it, by the way. It would put me in line for the throne and, suffice to say, I have even less desire for a wife and children than you do.' Benedict's smile turned sly. 'Does Moriana know she's the chosen one? Will you promise her your all? Faithful at last? I'd like to see that.'

'Perhaps you will.' Indifference was important when dealing with Benedict. Admitting weakness or desire was tantamount to handing him a sword to skewer you with.

'I'll tell Father you're courting with intent. He'll be thrilled.'

'I'm sure he will. Are you ever going to tell me why you're here? Run out of money? Still can't choose between the Cordova twins and their younger brother?'

'It's almost as if you know me.'

'I have work to do.' Theo reached for a pile of reports and dropped his gaze to the topmost.

'Father's dying.' Benedict's words came tightly furled, like little bullets that Theo hadn't seen coming until they hit. 'He found out two weeks ago that he has cancer and it's too advanced to treat. He's riddled with it. That's why he's dropping the petition—he can't follow through and take the Crown and I have no desire to. He's in hospital in France. I know you're not given to mercy, but he wants to come home.'

Theo sat back in his chair, reports forgotten, and gave Benedict his full attention. 'Your father's exile was self-imposed. He doesn't need my permission to return to Liesendaach.'

'He wants to come here. He wants to die in his childhood home.'

'No. That's not happening.' Dying or not, Constantine of Liesendaach was a dangerous adversary who'd never once stopped looking for ways to tear Theo down.

'It's not as if he wants the royal suite,' snapped Benedict. 'He's barely lucid. I'll provide the medical care and pick up the cost. All he wants is a room.'

'Then take him home with you.' Benedict had a townhouse in the city, provided by and paid for by the Crown. It wasn't a palace but it sure as hell wasn't a hovel.

Theo could see it now—an endless stream of visiting dignitaries and schemers coming to pay their last respects. People who hadn't graced the palace doors for years. Let Benedict deal with them; Theo would have none of it.

'What are you so afraid of?' Benedict taunted. 'You won. He lost. The world turns. So my father wasn't cut out to be King. Few are. He ruined the economy, so say some. He made too many deals in his own interest, so say others, and maybe they're right. He also raised you, fed and clothed you and never limited your education. He didn't *stop* you from doing anything. You wanted him gone; he *went*.'

'That's one version of his Regency,' Theo said acerbically. 'Would you like to hear mine?'

'*Yes.* I would. Because maybe then I could understand why you turned on us like a rabid dog the minute you took the Crown!'

Theo watched as his cousin turned away, his face red and his lips set in an ugly twist.

'I knew this for a fool's errand,' Benedict said into the deepening silence.

'Then why come?'

'Because he's my father. It's his dying wish to return to the place he calls home, and maybe, just maybe, he will find peace here.' Benedict leaned against the door frame, crossed his arms and employed a passable gimlet stare. 'He knows you think he orchestrated your family's death, even if he doesn't know who fed you the idea. He said to tell you that if he had done, you'd have been on that helicopter too.'

'I was supposed to be. Instead, I was skiving off with you. Horse racing, wasn't it? Your sure-fire winner you simply had to see race?'

'Lucky for you. Or would you rather have been on that flight?' Benedict smiled but it didn't reach his eyes. 'We were family once. I cared about you. Looked after you.'

Saved you.

To this day, Theo still didn't know if Benedict had acted in complete ignorance when he'd prevented Theo from getting on that flight, or whether he'd known what his father was up to and simply hadn't been able to stomach losing Theo. Whatever the reason, Theo had lived. His parents and brother had not.

And Benedict had ceased to be Theo's confidant.

'Leave the numbers for the doctors.'

'And what?' said Benedict. 'You'll monitor the situation? I left those numbers with your secretary two weeks ago, one week ago, and again yesterday. *Three times* I asked you to call me. Good thing I remember where you live.'

'I didn't receive any of those messages.'

'Then fire your secretary.'

'Was there anything else?' He'd had enough of this conversation.

'Yes. I won't be joining you and all the other righteous souls for dinner this week, or any other week in the foreseeable future. I would have let your staff know...if I thought the message would ever reach you. Don't set a place for me. Don't expect me to play the royal prince once my father is gone. I'm done.'

'You'll lose your title and your allowance.'

Benedict spread his arms wide. 'At least I'll be my own man. My position in this family is untenable. I've tried to get through to you. I can't. Nor am I willing to do what my father wants me to do. Time to move on.'

'I'll let my staff know.' Theo didn't want to feel sick to his stomach. There was no use wishing for a different outcome. 'By the way, Moriana knows you're here. She sends her regards.'

Benedict laughed. 'Poor little pedigree princess, always so proper. First Casimir and now you. I feel sorry for her. Maybe I should ask her if she wants to run away with me. She'd probably be better off.'

'I wouldn't advise it.'

'Then tell her I hope she enjoys her stay and regret that I must take my leave before renewing our acquaintance. There. Aren't we all so civil and grown-up?' Benedict bowed, a mocking salute. 'See you at the funeral. *Cousin.*'

He turned and made his exit, his long, angry stride echoing down the corridor.

Theo closed his eyes and banged his head softly against the padded headrest of the chair.

Of all the confrontations he'd ever had, dealing with Benedict had always been the hardest. He *wanted* to trust the man. They'd been close as children. Similar in age, similar in temperament, royals but not the heir apparent. Less had been expected of them and they'd lived up to that expectation and beyond.

Benedict *had* looked after him at times.

And sometimes, when his back was to the wall and the vultures were gathering, Theo still wanted Benedict at his side.

Theo was still sitting in his chair half an hour later. He'd done no work. Hadn't even glanced at the reports on his desk other than to leaf through them in search of a memo saying Benedict had called. If the information was buried in there somewhere, he hadn't yet found it. And then his deputy Head of Security knocked on the door frame. He'd asked the man to monitor Benedict's departure from the palace. Discreetly, of course.

'Has he gone?' he asked, and the older man nodded.

'Not before he found the visiting Princess and had a few words with her.'

'Was he civil?'

'Exceedingly, sire. The Prince told the Princess she was looking divine and said something to the effect that her broken engagement must be agreeing with her. She laughed and asked after his health and they talked a little about a painting they'd both bid for at auction but neither of them had won. He asked how long she was staying and she said a week. He bid her a pleasant stay, told her to make sure she saw the artwork in the southeast drawing room and then left.'

'Did I ask for a rundown on their conversation?'

'No, sire. My recount is probably wholly unimportant.'

'Wrong.' The information was extremely important. Benedict hadn't told Moriana about the petition being buried. He hadn't caused trouble. And that was unusual. 'Thank you. It's useful knowledge.'

The man nodded. 'I'm also here because you'd best be telling me what you want done regarding security for the Princess. Because she's just stationed the three men I put on her too far away to be of use and she didn't bring any security personnel of her own.'

'They'll be arriving this afternoon.' Augustus had insisted.

Theo picked up his desk phone and searched his mind for the internal number for the Queen's chambers. He thought it was zero zero two, but he couldn't be sure. It had been so long since he'd used it.

She picked up, and her voice was warm and relaxed as she said, 'Hello.' His Princess was in a far better mood than he was. Hopefully she'd stay that way when he overruled her security arrangements.

'You need to know what is and isn't going to happen, security-wise,' he told her curtly. 'There's a briefing in ten minutes. My security team will show you to my office.'

'Actually, I've just ordered tea brought to the most romantic little sitting room I've ever seen,' she said, the laughter in her voice a startling contrast to the encounter he'd recently had with his cousin. 'There's a huge vase of fragrant roses on the table, the sun is streaming in through the open windows and the breeze is sending the gauze curtains flying. I can smell the forest and I've just discovered a pair of armless white leather recliners which are either sunbeds or massage beds. Regardless, I'm currently lying on a cloud and your chances of getting me off it any time soon are…ooh, *nil*. More to the point, if this security discussion is about me and my needs I want it to happen here, in these quarters, so I can see for myself what you're proposing. I want you to walk me through it.'

Her words made sense, more was the pity. 'Be ready in five minutes,' he grated.

'I'll order more tea,' she said smoothly, and hung up on him.

His security deputy stood there, still largely oblivious to the force of nature Theo was about to unleash on their world. 'We're going to her.'

He was a good man, his security guard. Well trained. Because all he did was nod.

Theo's mood did not improve as Moriana negotiated her security requirements. He overrode most of her requests, acceded to two of them, and wore her contemplative stare in silence once the security team was back in place.

'Seems like overkill,' she said.

'My team is experienced. They'll only step in when needed.' He couldn't joke about security measures and he would never, ever downgrade them. 'I don't take risks. I do need to sleep at night, and I won't if I'm worried about the safety of the people under this roof. I can protect you, Moriana. But you need to let me.'

He wasn't negotiating.

Finally, she spread her arms wide. 'Okay.'

But he still didn't relax.

'Bear with me while I try and figure out what pitched your mood blacker than tar,' she said as she headed for the sunroom she seemed to like so much. 'Augustus gets like this. It's not always my doing but I'm not ruling it out. More tea?'

'No, thank you.'

'What did Benedict want?'

'Too much.' The words were out of his mouth before he could call them back. Then again, wasn't he supposed to be sharing his life with her? Trusting her with the complications of his court?

'So either you refused him and you're brooding about it or you agreed to do something you don't want to do,' she said. 'Which is it?'

'Do you think me cold?' he asked instead of answering her question.

'No.'

'Do you think me ruthless? Calculating?'

'Yes. Both. Show me a good ruler who isn't.'

'My uncle's dying,' he said.

Her eyebrows rose.

'He wants to spend his last days here at the palace.'

'Ah,' she murmured. 'And the petition for your removal? What's happening there?'

'Benedict says it's been abandoned.'

'Interesting. Do you believe him?'

Theo couldn't sit still beneath her carefully assessing gaze. He stood and crossed to the window but he could still feel her eyes on him like an itch between his shoulders. 'I don't know.'

'How long does your uncle have left?'

He didn't know that either, but apparently he had the doctor's contact details somewhere to hand. 'Got a phone?'

She disappeared through the doorway and came back moments later and handed it to him. It was gold-plated and disguised as a set of balance scales. He looked at the phone, looked back at her.

'If there's a less absurd phone around here, I've yet to find it,' she said. 'Why do you think I always sound so thoroughly cheerful when I answer it?'

Two minutes later, Theo had the contact details he needed. Two minutes after that he was speaking to his uncle's head physician in France. When he put the phone down ten minutes later he was armed with the knowledge that Benedict hadn't been exaggerating Constantine of Liesendaach's illness. The doctor had given Constantine days to live. Already, he was slipping in and out of consciousness as his body's organs began to fail. Constantine had refused life support assistance and Benedict had told the medical staff to honour the request. Palliative care only for the former Regent.

'We're talking days,' he said. 'Assuming he doesn't die in transit.'

'Okay. Now we know.' Her calm poise steadied him. 'Will you grant him a state funeral?'

'No.' He couldn't stomach giving that honour to a murderer. 'There can still be enough pomp to satisfy the burial of a former Prince Regent without gazetting it as such.'

'Do you seek my opinion on the matter?' she asked.

'Yes.' Why not? There was something grounding about the sheer practicality of her questions so far.

'Okay, here goes. You neutralised the man ten years ago but didn't exile him. Either before he dies or after, you're going to have to bring him home. You're going to have to try and make sense of his life and actions and then you're going to speak in public of human frailty, temptation and forgiveness, whether you mean those words or not. Do it now. Get it done. Show your people—and him—a strong king's mercy.'

She hadn't moved from the sofa but her words drew him away from the window and back around, such was her command of his attention. She sipped her tea, an island of serenity, and it dawned on him that she was extremely good at being someone's muse.

'Your uncle is no threat to you now. Benedict, bless him, is in the same boat as you in that he has no wife or heirs. Benedict won't challenge you. He *can't* challenge you. The throne is yours.'

She was good at this. 'I still need a queen.'

'And now you can take your time and search properly and find one who suits your needs.'

She was *right there in front of him*. How could she be so clear-eyed when it came to dealing with his uncle and cousin and not know she was the perfect candidate?

'How often does Augustus seek your counsel?' he asked.

'Almost daily, why?'

'You're good at it.'

She smiled wryly. 'I grew up listening to my father speak freely of state concerns at dinner each night. Not major concerns, nothing classified to begin with, but even as children we always had one topic of state to discuss, alongside the regular conversation about our days. He'd ask our opinions. Make us defend our positions. Showed us how to respectfully discuss problems and the fixing of them. They were lessons in statecraft.'

'And how old were you when you started this?'

'I hardly recall when it started, only that it was an everyday occurrence. My father always paid attention to my mother's voice. He relied on her for support and to bring fresh perspective to the table. When she died, so too did much of my father's enthusiasm for his role. It's one of the reasons he abdicated early, even if not the only one.'

She put down her teacup. 'I'm scaring you, aren't I? You're not used to dealing with women who expect a great deal of intellectual intimacy from their nearest and dearest.'

He wasn't used to dealing with *anyone* who expected intellectual intimacy from him.

'I did warn you,' she said.

'You did.' And, God, he wanted more of it. He ruled alone; he always had. But this…this effortless back and forward, argument and counterargument, not for argument's sake but with the clear aim of lifting a burden… He would have more of this.

'You're looking a little wild-eyed,' she said.

He'd just realised what he'd been missing all these years.

She rose and came to stand beside him, looking out over the gardens, following his lead and dropping the subject. 'What's that?' she asked, pointing towards a tiny cottage on the edge of the forest.

'It used to be my mother's painting studio. These days the gardeners use it as their headquarters.'

'Will you walk me there? Through the gardens?'

'Now?'

She nodded.

'You'll need a hat. And a shawl for your shoulders. Possibly an umbrella.'

She looked at him as if he amused her.

'What?' he said. 'It's a long way. You're fair-skinned. You'll burn.'

'I have dark hair, dark eyes, olive skin and when I encounter the sun I tan. Also, you're starting to sound like my mother.'

Her mother had been a tyrant.

'You do realise,' he murmured, 'that mothers are, on occasion, right?'

By the time they reached the outer doors of the palace there was a woman's sun hat, an umbrella and a gauzy cotton scarf waiting for them. Moriana sighed. Theo smiled. Heaven knows where his household staff had sourced them from.

First the scarf—Theo draped it around her neck and made a production of rearranging it several times until it completely covered her bare shoulders. Clearly he was more adept at taking a woman's clothes off than helping one put clothes on.

The hat came next. Then he offered her his aviator sunglasses. 'We should take water,' he said.

'It's a walk in the garden, not a mountain trek. Why are you being so…'

'…attentive?' he offered.

'I was going to say *weird*. I've been in gardens with you a dozen times over. Never before have you offered me a hat.'

'It wasn't my place. Ask me how often I wanted to offer you a hat. You wore one once. It was bright green, floppy-brimmed and had a red band with purple polka dots. You had your hair in a long plait that went halfway down your back and your hair ribbon matched your hat band.'

'I remember that hat,' she said. 'I don't remember the day you speak of.'

'Your brother dared you to fetch us some wine from the kitchens but you told him you already had two strikes against you and he'd have to get it himself because three strikes a day was your limit and you still had to get through your dance lesson.'

'Do you remember what my strikes were?'

'Apparently you'd chosen the wrong shoes for the right dress and embarrassed your mother in front of her friends. That was strike one. Strike two happened at lunch because you'd forgotten the name of someone's pet spaniel.'

'Oh.' One of *those* days. 'Good call when it came to me not stealing the wine, I guess.' Moriana drew the scarf more tightly around her shoulders. Criticism had shaped her days as a child. It had been constructive criticism, of course. But it had also been relentless and demoralising, and she'd crawled into bed and cried herself to sleep more nights than she cared to remember, convinced she was an utter failure at life, the universe and everything. 'I used to take criticism too much to heart. I still do.'

'But you're working on it. *Moriana First*, remember?' His smile was warm and his eyes more blue than grey today. 'I'd never seen you looking prettier, that day, mismatched shoes and all. Naturally I had to steal the wine myself and pull your hair when I returned. Heaven forbid you didn't notice my reappearance.'

'I remember now. You then proceeded to ignore me for the rest of your visit.'

'I was fourteen. You were the prettiest thing I'd ever seen. Your hat made me want to sneak beneath it and kiss you and the wine made me almost brave enough to do it. But you were already spoken for and I was still a good boy back then. Kissing you would have sparked an international incident involving parents. My father would have handed me my ass. Naturally, I ignored you for the rest of my visit.'

His words were sweet. His eyes were shielded by long, sweeping lashes several shades darker than his hair.

'And why are you telling me this now?'

'Because confession is good for the soul.' He slid her a smile that held more than a hint of the boy he'd once been. 'I still wish I'd done it.'

And then he ducked his head beneath the brim of her hat and kissed her swiftly on the cheek.

What was that for? She didn't say the words but her eyes must have spoken for her.

'You said you wanted romance,' he said.

'You can stop courting me now. You're free and clear, remember?'

'I know.' He shoved his hands in his pockets and fixed his gaze on the horizon, giving her a clear view of his strongly hewn profile. 'But maybe I want to court you anyway.'

CHAPTER SIX

LIESENDAACH WAS A treasure trove of loveliness, Moriana decided later that afternoon as she and Aury investigated the Queen's wardrobe facilities more thoroughly. Theo had retreated to his office for the afternoon and exploration had beckoned in his absence. Theo's mother's clothes had been removed, but the three empty rooms devoted to clothes storage, hat and shoe space and a cupboard-sized jewellery safe spoke of a woman who'd loved to dress up and had spared no expense when it came to indulging that passion.

'If I remember correctly, the late Queen of Liesendaach used to collect clothes,' said Aury. 'Period clothes. Centuries-old gowns once worn by the aristocracy. Venetian masks, Russian uniforms, everything. Want to go looking for them?'

One of the two security guards standing just within her line of sight coughed and Aury rolled her eyes before turning to look at him.

'You wanted to say something?' Aury asked the guard.

'Yes, ma'am. There's a costume collection on the third floor, right above us.'

'I didn't know this place had a third floor,' said Moriana.

'Storage only. There are no windows, Your Highness. But that's where you'll find the costume collection. There's a staircase up to it from the door on your far left. The one that looks like a regular cupboard door.'

'I love secret staircases. Makes me feel right at home,' said Aury, with a flirtatious glance in the guard's direction. 'What's your name, soldier?'

'*Aury,*' Moriana chided, with a glance that spoke of not seducing Theo's security force within five minutes of their arrival.

'But everything's so *pretty* here,' Aury said with another coquettish glance in the direction of the unwary. Come to think of it, the poor man appeared quite aware and looked to be holding up just fine. And yes. He was very pretty—in a rugged, manly kind of way. Fair-haired and light-eyed, like so many of Liesendaach's people, he was also large of frame and lean when it came to bodyweight.

'What's your name, soldier?' Moriana repeated Aury's question.

'Henry, milady.'

'Good sturdy name,' Aury said. 'We should keep him. He knows where things are.'

'Uh-huh.' Moriana opened the door he'd spoken of. Sure enough, a spiral staircase beckoned, up, up and up towards darkness.

'I'll need to call it in and go on ahead if you want to take a look.' This from Henry again, all security-wise and conscientious.

'Let's do it.'

Two minutes later Henry led the charge up the stairs. Aury let him get all of two steps ahead before she started ogling the man's backside with a pleased little sigh. 'After you,' Moriana told her lady-in-waiting drily.

'*Thank* you, milady.'

'You're incorrigible.' But Aury's obvious enjoyment of her surroundings fuelled her own. Nothing like a fairy tale castle to explore to pass the time.

They eventually reached the third floor. Henry switched on lights as he went and when they reached the top of the stairs he crossed to a bank of old-fashioned switches and flicked them on, one after another. The place lit up, one tennis-court-sized section at a time, to reveal row upon row of gowns and costumes stretching into forever.

'There's a ledger,' Henry said, pointing towards a long side table. 'I believe the costumes are organised by period and then colour.'

'Henry, what's with the superior knowledge of the costumes?' asked Aury.

'My mother was seamstress to the late Queen,' said handsome Henry. 'I spent a lot of days up here as a child.'

'Were you ever a centurion?' Aury wanted to know. 'A Knight Templar?'

Henry smiled but neither denied nor confirmed his tendency towards dress-ups as a child.

'What does your mother do now?' Moriana asked.

'She works as a palace chambermaid, Your Highness.'

Handy. 'I don't suppose she's working *now* and would like to join us up here?'

'Imagine what we could do with these,' said Aury.

'Charity exhibitions, loans to museums…' Moriana was thoroughly on board with investigating ways of making sure these costumes were *seen*.

'Liesendaach's little big book of heavenly dresses,' said Aury. 'For charity, of course.'

Aury flipped open the ledger and started scanning the index. 'Oh, my lord. Royal wedding gowns!'

'We could be here a while.' There wasn't a lot that was going to compete with a collection of royal wedding gowns through the ages.

'Henry, I'm forward. It's a terrible flaw, I know,' Moriana began, and Aury snickered and handsome Henry blushed. 'But I think it's time we met your mother.'

Theo found them two hours later. He'd spent the afternoon on the phone to various medical specialists, including his uncle's physician yet again. He'd organised transport. He'd spoken to Benedict. No way was he bringing his uncle home without Benedict accompanying the man and staying on until Constantine's death.

Benedict probably had whiplash from Theo's change of heart, but he hadn't said no. Instead, he'd offered subdued thanks, asked for the lower west wing to be placed at their disposal, and promised not to linger once his father passed on.

Theo had a knot in his stomach at the prospect of all three of them being under the one roof again, and a burning need for Moriana's company. Not to talk it out, the way he'd done earlier. This time he was looking solely for a distraction.

She didn't disappoint.

There she sat, a tiny general in butter yellow, wholly surrounded by clothes in every colour imaginable, and attended by two chambermaids, her lady-in-waiting, his Head of Household Staff and two royal guards.

'Theo!' Moriana coloured prettily when she saw him. 'How long have we been up here? We were just...er... planning an exhibition for your...er...'

'Consideration,' Sam murmured helpfully.

'Yes, indeed. For your consideration.' Moriana smiled.

'And the benefit to me would be...?'

'Immense,' she said. 'Think of the children.'

'I'd like four,' he said silkily, and watched her expression grow wary. 'Walk with me. Please. There's something I'd like to discuss.'

'Of course,' she murmured and, with a nod for those surrounding her, she followed him along the narrow walkway with costumes on either side.

'What is it?' she asked as they began their descent down the spiral steps towards the second floor.

'The press know you're here.'

'How?'

'How do they know anything? On the one hand, my reputation precedes me. On the other hand, you're you, freshly jilted and vulnerable, and they know I was at your charity auction last night. They can smell a story and they've already been in contact with my press secretary for a statement. I'm willing to let them speculate as to what I'm doing with you. What are you willing to do?'

'No comment?' She nibbled on her lower lip and he was hard pressed not to bend his head and join her. 'I think "no comment". I'm through with thinking the press will treat me well any time soon, and you've never thought of them as allies.'

Worked for him.

'Do you really want four children?' she asked.

'Why not?' The only number he didn't want was two. The heir and the spare.

He'd been the spare, forever in the shadow cast by his brother's bright light, and he'd never liked the dynamic.

'Do you want children?' He remembered her reply to Augustus.

'Would you still offer for me if I didn't?' She slid him a rueful glance. 'Don't answer that. Rhetorical question. I know full well you need heirs.'

'But do you want children?' he pressed.

'Yes,' she said quietly. 'And there's no medical reason why I can't have them. I'm still fertile.'

'Do you remember that conversation? The one at your place when we were younger?' All the children of neighbouring monarchs had been there. All the young crown princes—him, Augustus, Casimir and Valentine—along with Moriana and Valentine's sister. Moriana had been subject to a fertility test in the days beforehand and had ranted long and loud about women's rights and invasion of privacy. And then Valentine and his sister had revealed they too had been tested for fertility and a host of other genetic flaws. Casimir had then bleakly revealed he'd been subject to not one but two DNA paternity tests.

There'd been a question on everyone's lips after that, and it had nothing to do with fertility.

It had been Valentine who'd finally caved and asked if Casimir was his father's son.

The answer had been a sullen, scowling, 'Yes.'

'I still remember that conversation,' he murmured.

'So do I,' said Moriana. 'Is it wrong for me to breathe a sigh of relief now that Casimir's poisonous father is dead? Is it wrong for me to think that you'll have less to worry about once your uncle has passed, and that I really like the shape of this new world order? Because I do like it. It makes me feel hopeful for the future—and the future of any children I might have.'

'*We* might have.'

'So you're still courting me,' she said. 'I thought now your marriage problem has been solved we might go back to being adversaries.'

'I still need a wife. Liesendaach still needs a Queen and an heir. And I'm doing my very best to be open and trusting with you and, believe me, it doesn't come easy.' Damn right he was still courting her. 'I'm asking questions. I'm sharing my thoughts. I brought a personal problem to you earlier. Marriage may not be something I need quite so urgently, but it's still something I want. See? This is me—sharing and caring.'

'I…see,' she said dubiously. 'Well, then…good job.'

'And there you go again. Lying to me,' he said darkly. 'What *else* can I improve on?'

'I…' She spread her hands somewhat helplessly. 'Theo, I appreciate your efforts and the confidences you've shared with me today. Truly.'

'But you're still not taking my proposal seriously.'

'I am now.'

She looked at him uncertainly and he wished he could rid her of her insecurities.

'I'd even throw in your favourite wedding gown from upstairs.'

'They're all quite exquisite.'

But she didn't say yes.

'I wonder what Casimir's going to do about his daughter,' she said suddenly.

'Where did that come from?' Moriana was hard on his ego at times; he'd give her that. Moments ago he'd been offering up his innards for her perusal. Now she was talking about her former fiancé's daughter.

'I'm thinking about a king's need for an heir—you started it. Then I thought of Casimir. He'll claim his

daughter—he told me as much—but she's still illegiti-
mate. She'll never rule.'

'Did he say he was going to marry the mother?'

'No. He spoke of her only briefly, to say that everything was up in the air. But I get the feeling he cares
for her more than he's letting on. More than he let on to
me, at any rate.'

'You care for him.' Theo had never liked that thought.

'Yes, although perhaps never as romantically as I
should have. I feel for Casimir. For over twenty years I
thought I was to marry him. He has a six-year-old daughter he never knew he had. He may be considering taking a commoner—a foreigner—for a wife. He's burying
his father, who he had a difficult relationship with. And
now he's a king. I wouldn't want to be him.'

Moriana was well rid of him. 'His transition to the
throne is assured.'

'Do you think he'll have an easier time of taking up
the reins than you did?'

'He's older, wiser, and there's no other royal alternative waiting in the wings. The throne is his.'

'Will you help him? Counsel him?'

'If he asks for my counsel, yes.'

'Why did you never ask for help when you first took
the throne?'

Always with the difficult questions. 'Help from
whom? Byzenmaach? Casimir's father supported my
uncle as Regent; there was no help for me there. Thallasia stayed neutral until Valentine took the throne. Only
then could I look there for support and by then I was
through the worst of it. Your father was the only one to
ever offer the hand of friendship and even then I didn't
take it because I didn't trust him. I didn't trust anyone.'

'We know. It was one of those round-table conversations we had about you. My father thought you a wastrel, initially. In his defence, you had gone out of your way to give that impression.'

Theo smirked. 'I was hiding in plain sight.'

'But then you neutralised your uncle and began to undo the damage done and within six months my father was your biggest fan.' She slanted him a glance. 'Would it surprise you to know that another reason my brother took the throne early was so that *you* would have a regional ally you might trust?' Theo stopped walking. Moriana continued her stroll along the corridor before finally looking over her shoulder. 'Do keep up.'

He had no words. His day had been full of too many surprises already. 'Who *are* you?'

'I'm Moriana of Arun, sister to a King, daughter to a King, and potentially your future Queen.'

'I need a drink.'

'I concur. How about you walk me to a bar?'

He turned her around and walked her to his rooms instead. They were closer and there was a bar in there. It wasn't fully stocked, but all his favourites were present and hers could be delivered.

'Is now a good time to let you know that if we marry I'll be wanting full access to Liesendaach's education, healthcare and arts portfolios, and I wish to be kept apprised of the regional water resources plans?' she asked.

'Tomorrow would be a better time to hit me with that,' he muttered. 'I'm surprised Augustus is willing to let you go, what with all you do.'

'Needs must.' They'd reached his rooms and he stepped back to let Moriana enter before him. 'Although, in the interest of full disclosure, there is the small matter of my overdrawn bank account,' she said dulcetly. 'He's not particularly happy about that.'

'What did you buy?' Augustus had never mentioned his sister being a frivolous spender. He was more likely to gripe about her inability to stop buying and selling major artworks.

'A tapestry. It was one of ours from long ago. My great-grandfather sold it and seven others like it. Together they told a story of love, war and an abandoned child who grew to be a great warrior and mistakenly fell in love with his mother, at which point he put a sword through her heart and then fell on his own. Sword, that is.'

'Happy. I can see why you had to have it back.'

'Yes, well, unfortunately, the original set was split between several buyers. My grandmother bought the first one back; my mother recovered three more. Augustus found one. I found two more. The last remaining seller knew their tapestry would complete the set and priced accordingly. I paid up and Augustus froze my spending account until June next year.'

She sounded amused rather than put out. 'Quite a good time for me to consider marriage, all things considered. I *will* have a spending account as your Queen, right?'

'Yes, but you'll have to answer for it.'

'I always do.' She crossed the room to look out of his window. 'You keep horses here.'

'We breed horses here. Warhorses for Liesendaach's mounted guard regiment.'

Moriana hummed her approval. '*Very* nice.'

She was biting back a smile and he crossed to her side and looked out. His stable master was supervising the unloading of horses from a livestock transport truck into the courtyard below. Three big greys and a tiny black Shetland stallion were being introduced to several stable hands.

'Is there anything here that's not pretty?' she asked, and he remembered an overheard conversation about stable boys and lustful thoughts.

'You'd best be looking at my horses, Princess, and not my stable hands. And I suggest you avoid entirely the company of royal horsemen stationed here.'

Moriana's smile turned positively beatific. 'You have a company of royal horsemen stationed here? How did I not know this? I need to tell Augustus.'

She wanted to torture Augustus with visions of her sleeping her way through Liesendaach's mounted regiment, most likely. The problem was, Theo couldn't admit to overhearing that conversation between her and her brother because then all hell would break loose. He didn't want all hell to break loose right now. He wanted to relax and regain some small sense of control and maybe, just maybe, get her to look at him the way she'd looked at him last night and then again this morning.

'Have you ever just wanted a day to be over?' he asked.

'You mean how I felt most of yesterday and the day before?'

'Point.'

'Are you thinking about your uncle?'

'And Benedict. And you. And the future and what to make of it.' And trust and how to build it with this woman.

'No wonder you need a drink. Weighty topics all.'

And connected all, for together they did—or would—make up his family unit.

Moriana turned, her back to the window now, as she stood before him. At least her attention was no longer being diverted by his horsemen. 'Of course you don't have mindless sexual conquests to distract yourself with any more. What a shame.'

'Moriana, I'm going to strangle you soon,' he warned.

A mischievous smile lit her face. 'Are you ready to teach lesson two? I'm ready for lesson two.'

'Breath play? I doubt it.'

She blinked.

He smiled. 'Was that not what you meant?'

'I…er…no. Definitely not what I meant. Baby steps, Theo. It's only lesson two.'

'A lesson that isn't scheduled until tomorrow.'

She sighed. 'Guess I'll have to keep looking at all the pretty horses…and their handlers.'

On the other hand, it wasn't as if he had anything better to do. He could use a little distraction. And there was something to be said for physical release as a means of easing tension.

'Would you like to keep looking at my stable hands?' he murmured. 'Because hands on the windowsill if you would.'

'Oh, no. No.' She quickly put distance between her and the window, before turning to keep him in sight. 'I know what "hands on flat surfaces" involves. We covered that lesson this morning, and we are not doing it again in front of a window with your men looking on. That's lesson eight hundred and sixty-five *thousand*. Not to mention a very bad idea.'

'Or you could sit on the bed.'

One moment she was railing at him, eyes wide. The next minute she was perched on the end of his bed, arms crossed in front of her.

'I have a request,' she said.

He expected nothing less.

'I'd like you naked this time,' she said.

'As you wish.' Theo smiled, the focus firmly back on him as he stalked towards the bed. 'Perhaps you could undress me.'

Moriana tucked her hands a little higher beneath her arms. 'I didn't expect these lessons to require quite so much initiation on my part.'

'Live and learn. You could start with my buttons if my belt's too intimidating.'

'I refuse to be intimidated. I can do this. I want to do this.'

'That's the spirit.'

She started with his belt buckle, her touch deft and light. By the time she had his fly undone he was hard beneath the brush of her hands and he was the one unbuttoning his shirt, because bravery should be rewarded.

She leaned in and closed her eyes and set her cheek to the skin just above the low ride of his underwear, and when she turned her head the better to taste skin he clenched his hands into fists instead of sliding them through her hair and guiding her actions. If the last lesson had been about Moriana surrendering control of her body to him, he wanted this lesson to be about her taking control and keeping it, exploring it. And for that he had to ease off on his.

He shouldered his shirt to the floor and she looked up as if he was offering the finest of feasts after a lifetime of starvation. He wished she had more experience but he wasn't ever going to let her get it from anyone else. She'd had her chances and hadn't taken them.

She took her time when it came to getting his trousers off. He took his time laying her on the bed and stretching out beside her. She liked looking at him, when he wasn't distracting her with kisses, deep and drugging. She liked touching him and he encouraged it.

'What's the lesson?' she asked again, so he named one.

'Rubbing,' he whispered. 'Rocking.' Until they drove each other mad. 'No penetration.' He hadn't done this since his teens. 'Easy.'

He wrapped his arm around her waist and hauled her on top of him, knees to either side of his hips, and if that wasn't giving her full control he didn't know what would.

'Should I take my clothes off?'

'Your call.' Her dress was soft and her panties felt like silk against his erection. Hot wet silk.

The panties came off and her dress stayed on as she positioned herself over him again, and slowly settled against him.

'I like feeling you against me,' she murmured against his lips and he closed his eyes and tried to think of anything but the feel of warm wet womanhood against him. Slowly she began to rock against him, her hands either side of his head. 'Like this?'

'Yes.' Sliding his hands beneath her dress, up and over the globes of her buttocks, the better to position her for maximum drag over sensitive areas.

She was slick enough for both of them and for the most part he let her find her way, only sliding his hand around to rest his thumb against her once or twice to begin with until she arched up to a sitting position, grabbed his hand by the wrist and held it there.

She closed her eyes and her trembling increased as he used every trick he'd ever learned to make it good for her.

'Do you close your eyes the better to imagine someone else?' he grated, because he could be cruel and tender in equal measure and because she'd said the same to him.

'Put it in,' she whimpered. 'Theo, please. Fill me. Put it in.'

'Not until we're married.'

'Since when has this been one of your conditions for bedding a woman?' Disbelief coloured her voice but her body still moved and so did his.

'Since you.' He rolled her over and wrapped her legs around him and added his weight and a sinuous roll to the negotiations; it had been years since he'd been this close to coming with such minor stimulation, but this was Moriana and her abandon had always fuelled his. 'I will put my mouth on you and my hands, do this all day long, take you to the edge and make you wait, but you only get me in you when you're mine.' Which begged the question... How long did it really take to arrange a royal wedding? Because the restraint was killing him.

'I hate you.' But her hands were in his hair and she was drawing his head down into a kiss so hot and desperate that the groan he heard was his.

'You want me.'

'Yes,' she sobbed. 'Theo, I'm—'

Coming, and so was he, all over her stomach, messing her up, painting her his.

She was too responsive. 'You came again, I don't care what you say. I win.'

She laughed a little helplessly.

'You know, simultaneous satisfaction is quite a feat. Very rare.'

'Is it? I wouldn't know.'

'It's rare.'

She studied his face, her eyes searching and solemn. 'You're still courting me.'

'Yes, and I fully intend to win you. How much plainer do I have to make it?'

'I have a temper,' she said next.

'Pent-up passion has to go somewhere.'

'I have high standards. I'm hard on myself and on others. I'll be hard on you if you fail me.'

'I'd expect nothing less. If I think you're being too hard on either yourself or others I'll call you on it. We'll argue and your passion will go somewhere.'

'I can be a workaholic.'

'Liesendaach needs a lot of work.'

'You're not the slightest bit self-conscious about lying here naked, are you?'

'Should I be?'

She sighed and shook her head. 'No. Your body is flawless.' She dropped her gaze below his waist. 'And very well proportioned. I never realised that shameless-ness could be quite so enticing.'

He was comfortable in his skin. She, on the other hand, still had her dress on. 'I would see you comfort-able in your skin before we're through,' he told her. 'Es-pecially in private.'

'More lessons.' The curve of her lips was captivating and always had been.

'Yes, many more lessons, starting now. Take your dress off.'

'But...aren't we done for now?'

'I promised to keep you strung out on the edge of release for hours,' he reminded her silkily. 'I need to keep my word.' She had a very sensitive neck. It re-sponded well to lips and tongue and the faintest graze of his teeth.

'I think you're overestimating my resistance to your touch,' she murmured as she arched beneath him.

Twenty minutes later and after two orgasms, ripped from her body in rapid succession, Princess Moriana of Arun told him to stop.

'Have I persuaded you to marry me yet?'

'Not yet,' she murmured with a thoroughly satisfied smile. 'But full points for trying.'

CHAPTER SEVEN

MORIANA CRACKED ONE eye open to the sound of cutlery landing on a table. She was in Theo's room, in Theo's bed, wholly naked, but the man himself wasn't there. Instead, a chambermaid was busy setting a dinner table in the room next door. Moriana could see bits of her every now and again through the half-closed door and the reflection on the window. It was dark outside and dark in the room she'd been sleeping in. The adjoining room looked as if it was lit by candlelight.

Perhaps it was.

She'd been schooled, she remembered that much. She remembered Theo playing her body the way a master violinist played a foreign instrument. Paying attention, learning what worked and what didn't, down to the tiniest detail, and adjusting his attentions accordingly. He'd played her to perfection. He'd known what she wanted before she did and kept her waiting.

He still hadn't bedded her fully.

And now she was in a strange room with no clothes to wear other than stained ones, and no idea what to do next. The maid finished her preparations and slipped from view and Moriana took the opportunity to escape into the bathroom. A shower later, she entered his dressing room and took one of his shirts from its hanger and put it on. It was of the softest cotton and fell to the tops of her thighs. She found her panties and put them on too.

She tried not to think about what she looked like but there were mirrors on three walls and in the end it was inevitable that she would meet her reflection. Make-up gone and hair untended, she barely recognised herself. In her eyes was an awareness of pleasure. On her skin were faint marks left by the press of strong hands and a hot, sucking mouth. Theo hadn't treated her like a princess. He'd treated her like a woman fully capable of pleasing herself and, in doing so, pleasing him.

She took a blue two-tone tie from his collection and used it as a hairband, and now she looked all carefree and confident.

Looked, not felt. Because she'd never felt quite so laden with doubt.

She'd only ever repressed the more passionate side of her nature and here she was feeding it, and Theo was nothing if not encouraging. With him at her side she was slowly eroding the self-control she'd fought for all her life—the control her family valued above all else.

'You're screwed,' she told the woman in the mirror, and then turned her back on her and there stood Theo. Watching. The hawk in the granary.

'Not yet,' he said, and straightened as she approached. 'What is it you think I can't give you?' His eyes were sharp, more grey than blue in this light.

'There doesn't appear to be anything you can't deliver.'

He was still watching her so she sent him a smile to back up her words.

'Don't do that,' he said.

'Do what?'

'Retreat behind your mask of cool politeness. It

doesn't work when you're wearing nothing but my shirt.' His gaze slid to her face. 'And my favourite tie.'

'Is it really your favourite tie?'

'It is now.' She needed to get used to Theo's lazy compliments and the intensity of his gaze. 'Dinner's ready. It's the romance portion of the evening. I added candles.'

He turned away and she followed him into the adjoining room. 'So I see.' The room was bathed in soft light and shadows and the table was set for two. A nearby balcony door stood open and she could smell the scent of the forest and feel the lingering heat of the day in the air.

'I love it here.' It wasn't like the palace she'd grown up in, heavy on grey stone and small, defensible windows. This palace had been built for openness and sensual delight and showing off its beauty. It made her feel wide open to possibilities in a way that her home palace never had.

Or maybe it was the man currently pulling her dining chair out for her who was doing that.

His loose weave shirt was a dove-grey colour and unstarched. His trousers were khakis and he hadn't got around to putting on shoes.

'I got your meal preferences from the Lady Aury and took the liberty of sending them to my kitchen staff,' he said. 'We have our own regional specialities, of course, and tonight I thought we could try a mix of both your preferences and mine. See how well they mesh. The serving staff will come to the door. We can take it from there.'

A soft ping of a bell prevented her from answering. Theo went to the door and came back with a trolley laden with dome-covered dishes. There were scallops, fish stew or soup of some sort, duck salad with a pomegranate dressing—one of her favourites—and there was Mediterranean salad, heavy on the olives—which was perhaps a favourite of his. There was baked bread and lots of it.

'Fish stew and sourdough. Messy but worth it,' he said.

She took the bowl of stew he handed her and passed him the bread basket in return. 'Do you dine in here often?' she asked.

'More often than I should,' he answered. 'There's a family dining room, of course. It hasn't been used for years. Not since my uncle's rule.'

'Where did your family dine? You know—before.'

Before the helicopter crash that had cost them their lives. 'My mother used to enjoy dining on the west terrace on warm summer nights. In winter there was a modest dining room with a large fireplace that we used a lot. I don't use either any more. Too many ghosts and there are so many other rooms to choose from.'

'Do you ever get lonely here?'

'There are people everywhere,' he said by way of an answer and, yes, they were his people but they weren't family or loved ones; they were employees. He'd lost two families, she realised. One in a terrible accident and the other when he'd taken the throne and stripped his uncle of power. No wonder he kept to himself and found it hard to contemplate having loved ones he could rely on.

'I took your advice. Benedict and my uncle will be arriving tomorrow or the next day, depending on my uncle's condition,' he said. 'It may not be fun. I'm considering sending you home until it's done.'

Moriana put her fork down and her hands in her lap. Hands were revealing. And she was suddenly nervous. The food she'd been enjoying suddenly sat heavy in her stomach. She didn't have the right clothes on for a farewell speech. More to the point, she'd only just got here and didn't want to go. They'd been making progress, of a sort. Working each other out, learning each other's strengths and weaknesses, and she wanted that to continue because it was challenging and fun and the sex was flat-out fantastic, and did he really expect her to get a taste of that and then just *leave*? Because that was inhumane.

'Of course.' She couldn't look at him.

And then she did look at him, and it wasn't just lust she felt. She also had the strong desire to comfort him and be with him so he didn't have to go through this alone. 'Unless, of course, you think I might be of use to you here. I could stay if you thought that. I've been through the death of a family member before. I know how it goes and what to do. Of course, so do you.'

'I'm trying to spare you, not push you away.' His voice was soft and deep and utterly compelling. 'Would you rather stay?'

'If you—'

'No,' he said gently. '*Moriana First*, remember? You're turning over a new leaf. What do *you* want to do?'

'I want to stay and be of use,' she said, and meant it. She wanted to be with him, stand by him.

'And would you like the lessons and the romance and my awkward moments of oversharing to continue?' he asked, and there was no more denying that he was turning her into a believer of all things Theo.

'Yes.' She nodded, and reached for more bread so she wouldn't reach for him. 'Yes, I would.'

Benedict and his father arrived the following morning. They were put in the west wing, out of the way, no visitors allowed, and Moriana stayed out of their way. Benedict did not dine with them—she didn't see him for two days—but on the morning of the third day he ventured into the garden and when he saw her he headed her way.

He looked haggard and sleep-deprived, but the reason for it was obvious. His father was dying. Theo was ignoring him. This family was a fractured one, and she didn't know what to make of it.

'You were right about the artwork here,' she said when he reached her. 'It really is extraordinary.'

'I know. My ancestors have done us proud. This place. These gardens.' He smiled faintly and looked around. 'There's nothing quite like them.'

'How's your father?'

'Asleep. That's the easy word for what he's doing. Better than unconscious or comatose. The journey here knocked him around, but he knew he was home. He recognised it.'

'Does your father ask for anyone?'

'No.'

'Has Theo seen him yet?'

'No.' Benedict smiled grimly. 'I doubt that's going to happen.'

'Have *you* caught up with Theo yet?'

'Briefly.' Benedict shoved his hands in his pockets as they started walking and she fell into step beside him. 'Not that there was a lot of catching up involved. We haven't been close for years.'

'I heard that.'

'Theo wasn't always like he is now,' said Benedict. 'He was more open as a child. More inclined to let people in. Then his family died, and that dimmed him a lot but he was still accessible. Still him. It was a couple of months after his twenty-third birthday that everything changed between him and me—between him and everyone—and it was like a wall went up overnight and it was twenty feet high and made of obsidian and there was no way to scale it.'

Moriana said nothing.

'God knows I'm not without flaws,' Benedict muttered. 'But they'd never bothered him before. These days I like to think I've got a better handle on those flaws.'

'Do you care for him?' she asked quietly.

'I used to. He was like a brother to me. Now he's a stranger and I'm here under sufferance. Once my father is dead and buried I'll choose a new life and walk away from this one. It's time.'

She'd voiced a similar sentiment only days ago. The circumstances were different but the dream to simply walk away from a life of royal duty was a vivid one at times. Hard to say how it would work in reality. No one she knew had ever been bold enough or weary enough to try.

'You're his closest blood relative. Second in line to the throne. He could use your support.'

Benedict snorted softly. 'Theo doesn't want my support. I've already offered it too many times to count. By the way, this State Dinner tomorrow night that I can no longer avoid—I'm bringing a date. One of the Cordova twins.'

She narrowed her gaze and shot him a sideways glance. 'Why would you do that? To make Theo uncomfortable or to make me uncomfortable?'

'Two birds, one stone,' he said, and then shrugged as if in half-hearted apology. 'Would you believe it wasn't my idea? I owe the Cordovas a favour. They called it in.' Benedict held her gaze. 'Don't be jealous, Moriana. Theo's Theo. He has history with half a dozen women who'll be there tomorrow night, none of whom he ever wanted for his Queen. That list only ever had your name on it. You win. You both win.'

'He…had a list?'

'He had a wish. Why is this news to you? My cousin has never been able to take his eyes off you, even as a kid. He's yours. He always has been.'

'But…'

'Let me guess. His marriage proposal was framed as pure politics.'

'His marriage proposal was a form letter with my name filled in at the top and his signature at the bottom.'

Benedict laughed long and hard.

Moriana glared, until a reluctant tug lifted her lips. 'I hate humour. I'm a serious soul and why can't people just *tell me things*?' she muttered, and set Benedict off all over again.

'Seriously, go easy on my date,' Benedict said when finally he caught his breath. 'You're hard to compete with.'

'You mean I'm the perfect Ice Princess? Because, you've probably been too preoccupied to read the papers but that particular image is swiftly becoming tarnished. This morning I'm apparently intent on black-mailing Theo into marrying me by being pregnant with his triplets.'

Benedict's gaze skidded to her flat stomach. 'Congratulations?'

'Oh, shut it. It's pure fabrication.'

'You don't say.' And then he was grinning again. 'Tomorrow you should tell them they're mine.'

'Tomorrow I'll probably be brawling in public with a Cordova twin. I don't share well.' She chewed on her lip. 'You might want to forewarn her that I'm not feeling merciful.'

'If I do that her twin will want to come along as backup. Not to mention their brother.'

'I'll see to it that two more places are set for you and your friends. I may as well deal with them all at once.'

'You're fearless.'

'So I'm told.'

'Also slightly scary.'

'Spread that thought,' she said encouragingly.

They walked some more in companionable silence, and then Benedict spoke again. 'Moriana, a favour, if you please. If you do mean to invite all the Cordovas to dinner, seat Enrique next to me—as my partner. Because he is. In every sense.'

Oh. 'Oh, I see.' No wonder Benedict didn't want the throne. The fight required to accommodate his partner of choice would be enormous. 'Does Theo know?'

'He knows I enjoy both men and women, yes. I doubt he knows that I've finally made my choice. It's been made for years. Hidden for years.'

Oh, again. 'Does your father know?'

'No.'

'And yet you still want the Cordova brother at your side tomorrow night rather than wait until your father's dead? Why?'

'Because I'm burning bridges. I've no wish to be King and this is the strongest message I can send to those who might be inclined to rally around me after my father's death. Because Enrique thinks I'm ashamed of him and I'm sick of being that man. I don't care any more what anyone thinks. I love Enrique. I can't imagine my life without him in it. End of story.'

'Well, in that case, an invitation for Enrique and his

sisters can be with them this afternoon,' she murmured. 'I'm game if you're sure.'

'I'm sure.'

'You realise you should be having this conversation with Theo rather than me?' she asked him.

'I can't talk to a wall.' He turned on a smile that nearly blew Moriana away with its wattage. 'I've decided I like you, Princess. You're easy to talk to, you're smart and I suspect you're very kind. You're also very beautiful. Theo chose well for Liesendaach.' He stopped in front of her, heels together, and reached for her hand before bowing low and brushing her knuckles with his lips. 'A favour for me; now it's my turn to do a favour for you. Never forget—no matter who comes at you from Theo's past and tries to make you doubt him—never forget that he chose you. He even seems willing to change his ways for you.'

'You don't know that,' she said raggedly, no matter how much she suddenly longed to believe it. 'You don't know him any more.'

'I have my sources. Besides, I still have eyes. He still watches you as if there's no one but you in the room. He's watching you now.'

She looked around the garden and back towards the palace, where the guards stood stationed. Theo stood with them, hands in the pockets of his trousers. 'How long has he been there?'

'A few minutes, maybe a few more,' Benedict answered obligingly. 'I don't think he likes you walking with me. Hence the kiss.'

'What are you, five years old? How is annoying him going to help your cause?'

'It won't. But it does amuse me. Shall I walk you back to him?'

'Only if you're going to play nice.'

'Ah, well.' Benedict's amusement hadn't dimmed. 'I was heading to the stables anyway. Your Highness.' He bowed again. 'The pleasure was all mine.'

'You're a rogue.'

'Runs in the blood.'

'You realise I'll more than likely relay our conversation to Theo, word for word.'

'I never would have guessed.'

Benedict smiled as he walked away and she knew that look, even if she'd never seen it on this particular face before.

Do try and keep up, Moriana. You're my conduit to my cousin.

That was the point.

'What did he want?' asked Theo when she joined him. His eyes were flinty and his jaw was hard, and if he thought she was going to be their messenger girl he could think again.

'He wanted to talk to you. Apparently I'm the next best thing. The Cordovas are coming to the State Dinner tomorrow night. All of them, and it's going to be interesting.' She snaked her hand around his neck, with every intention of drawing his lips down towards hers. 'Are you angry with him for waylaying me?'

'Yes.'

'Are you angry with me for letting myself be waylaid?'

His lips stopped mere centimetres from her own. 'Yes.'

'Scared I'll like him?'

Theo's lips tightened. 'He can be charming.'

'I like you more.' She closed the distance between

their lips, not caring who saw them. She closed her eyes and stroked the seam of his lips until he opened for her. He was as ravenously hungry for her as she was for him and the thought soothed her soul even as it inflamed her senses. His arm was a steel band around her waist, the hardness between his legs all the encouragement she needed to continue.

And then one of the nearby guards cleared his throat. 'Photographers,' he said, and Theo's palm cupped her face protectively as he eased them out of the inferno of their kiss.

'Sorry,' she whispered, her confidence evaporating as he escorted her inside.

'Don't be. Think of the headlines. There'll be a love triangle. That or Benedict and I will be sharing you. Either way, you can expect a stern talking-to from your brother. So can I, for that matter.'

Moriana sighed. 'Welcome to my world.'

'I like your world, Princess. And I sure as hell like having you in mine. Don't overthink it.'

And he kissed her again to make sure she wouldn't.

The papers the following morning did not disappoint. *Claimed*, one headline ran, with a trio of pictures directly below it. Theo and Moriana just before that kiss, lips close and tension in every line of their bodies. Then the kiss itself, and it made her hot just to look at because it was a kiss better kept for the bedroom. Her family would despair of her. The third picture had Theo in full protective mode, his hand on her face and her head turned towards his shoulder as he glared at whoever had taken the picture. Mine, mine and *mine* that glare said.

That one she liked.

'Oh, message *received*,' Aury said when she saw the

headline and the pictures. 'That man is going to peel the skin off the flesh of anyone who tries to hurt you. It's even better than the picture of him butt naked. Your future king just bared his soul for you, and he did it for all to see.'

'What do you see?' Moriana snatched the paper back from the other woman. 'What soul?'

'It's there in every line of his body. His focus, the *want* in that kiss, the protection. Oh, this one's going on the fridge.'

'What fridge?' Moriana still couldn't see past her own surrender. 'What soul?'

'That man is totally committed. I knew it!' Aury was beaming. 'This isn't *just* the royal wedding of a generation...this is a love match.'

'Wait! What wedding? No! I'm not in love. I barely know the man. This is a...a sex match, if we ever get around to having sex. And it's convenient.'

'To have a husband who is head over heels in love with you, yes, it's very convenient.' Aury was practically dancing around the room. 'Henry, did you see this?'

'Yes, ma'am.'

'Henry, how many times do I have to tell you to call me Aury?'

Henry smiled with his eyes but his face remained impassive. 'Ma'am, I'm on duty. There are protocols.'

'But we *can* still solicit your opinion on the headlines, yes? It's a matter of state and safety and stuff.' Aury waved her hand in the air, possibly to encapsulate all the stuff she wasn't saying.

'The King knows what he's doing, ma'am.'

'See?' Aury whirled back around to face Moriana. 'Henry thinks Theo's in love.'

'That wasn't what he said.' Moriana did a little hand

waving of her own. 'I need new guards. And I definitely need a new lady-in-waiting.'

'You're right. I'm not waiting any more,' Aury declared. 'You're done. Gone. Claimed by a man who will move heaven and earth for you. It's my turn now.' She glanced at Henry from beneath her lashes.

'Henry,' said Moriana. 'Run.'

'Sorry, Your Highness, but I can't.' Henry looked anything but sorry. 'I'm on duty.'

'Do you want her back?' Theo asked Augustus, neighbouring King and brother of one Moriana of Arun. 'Because she's been here four days and I've lost control of my palace staff, my press coverage and the plot,' said Theo into the phone. He was staring down at the paper and wondering if Moriana was going to speak to him any time soon. *Claimed!* was the headline, and then there were pictures. And the pictures were revealing. Theo wanted to find a hole in the ground and bury himself in it.

Some things were meant to be common knowledge. His dangerous growing infatuation with Moriana was not one of them.

'She's a Combat General in a sundress,' he moaned.

'And you've *claimed* her,' Augustus said smugly. 'Enjoy.'

'You're looking at exactly the same paper as I am, aren't you?'

'When can I post the banns?' How could Augustus sound even more smug?

'I'm working on it. She's invited the Cordova twins and their brother to dinner, at Benedict's request. I'm taking it as a declaration of war on my past.'

'Reasonable call.'

'I don't often ask for advice,' Theo began.

'You've never asked for advice,' Augustus said drily.

'What should I do?'

'Why, Theo, you sit back and enjoy the tempest that is Moriana proving a point. You have to remember, *you wanted to let her run hot!*'

'You're saying this is my fault?'

'I'm saying you wanted it; you've got it.'

'She sent my dying uncle a book of prayer and a book about war.'

'Very subtle. You've already neutralised him. She's simply making sure he sees no avenue of counter attack through her. I imagine that's what inviting the Cordovas will be about too. Moriana's not one for extended torture. She'll give them a hearing, try to get them to reveal their hand, and if she doesn't like what's in it she'll cut them off at the wrist. Your role in this endeavour is to watch and learn what it's like to have my sister in your corner when enemies are present. Should you be foolish enough to reminisce with either of the delectable Cordova twins, you will lose your balls.'

Theo snorted.

'This is Moriana unleashed, remember? What could possibly go wrong?' said Augustus, with the blithe disregard of a man who knew he'd be elsewhere that evening. 'By the way, I'll be sending Moriana's dowry to you by the usual method. Meaning three hundred matched black cavalry horses and their riders will escort the dowry from my palace to yours—in full ceremonial garb.'

'I—what dowry?'

'Didn't she mention it? It's quite considerable. Paintings, linens, jewels, a regiment or two. It'll take the cavalry just under a month to get to you and I suspect Moriana will want to ride with them part of the way.

They should aim to reach your palace one week before the wedding, unless the Liesendaach cavalry decides to meet them at your border. You've met us at the border before, by the way, some three hundred years ago when Princess Gerta of Arun married Liesendaach's good King Regulus. If that happens it may take them all a little longer to reach you on account of all the jousting and swordfights that will likely take place along the way. I've been reading up on royal wedding protocol.'

'You're telling me you want *six hundred* steeds and riders prancing through *my* countryside for two weeks. Guarding *linen*?'

'And you thought Arunians were stern and resoundingly frugal.' Augustus was enjoying this. Theo was mildly horrified to find his reckoning of Augustus's character all wrong. 'Theo, I've already had six meetings with my highest advisors on how to honour Moriana properly should she ever decide to marry you. We will be parting with one of our most revered national treasures. If I had elephants I'd be sending them.'

'Elephants?'

'And now you're repeating my words. My work here is done. Good luck at dinner. Remember, do not take your eyes from the prize. Not that you ever do.'

'You're enjoying this too much.'

'I am. And there's more, and it needs to be said. If ever you want my advice regarding your beloved future wife, just call. I have the experience to help you through. Soon-to-be brother, I am here for you.'

Theo hung up on him.

Never again would he call Augustus of Arun for advice. Never, *ever* again.

CHAPTER EIGHT

MORIANA PREPARED FOR Liesendaach's State Dinner with the same kind of care she gave to any new social situation. She dug into the history of those attending, noted their interests and successes and their relationships to each other, memorised names, and dug deeper into anyone she thought might pose a problem. The information file on the people attending this dinner was already three hundred pages long, not including the staff, for she would have her eyes on them too, looking for areas of improvement.

Aury was on deck to guide her clothing choices and so too was the sixty-four-year-old former seamstress to Theo's mother and mother to bodyguard Henry. Of late, Letitia Hale had been a chambermaid and palace function assistant, which was, to Moriana's way of thinking, a regrettable waste of palace resources that she would see rectified. Letitia had a lifetime of service to call on and the inside knowledge Moriana needed when it came to what palace guests would be wearing.

Wise Owl Counsel, Aury called her. 'We need her,' she said, and Moriana agreed.

Henry just called her Mother.

'This evening I need to outshine the Cordova twins

and every other woman Theo has ever bedded,' Moriana told them.

'An admirable goal; I'm all for it,' said Aury. 'But we don't have half your jewellery here. Intimidation by necklace is going to be difficult.'

'Let's start with the gown. What did I bring?'

'Forest-green, floor-length and backless?' Aury disappeared into the dressing room and returned moments later with the garment. It was another one from Moriana's love-it-but-never-wear-it collection.

'Did you bring *anything* I normally wear?'

'Ah...'

'What *did* you bring?'

'The silver gown that makes you look like a fairy tale villain. Your favourite black gown—always a winner. The beaded amber with the ivory chiffon.'

'Can we see that last one?' said Letitia. 'Please?'

Aury brought it forward.

'Yes,' said Letitia. 'That one. The dining room is decorated in ivory with amber and silver accents. The tables are polished walnut, the floors a shade darker; the tableware has blue accents. The gown will play to all of those colours. Plus, the beading on that dress is magnificent.'

It was and there was no denying it. The strapless bodice was beaded, the fall of the chiffon skirt inspired. Back in Arun she'd have felt overdressed but it was the type of gown this palace called for. Elegant yet showy too, no apologies. Moriana had never worn it before, had never had to choose jewellery to match. Aury had not been remiss when it came to packing jewellery to go with the gown. The coffers of Arun didn't *have* any jewellery to match this one.

'The amber beaded gown it is,' she said. 'What jewellery *did* we bring? And if we brought sapphires let's ignore them. I'd rather not match the tableware.'

'Why did we not pack rubies?' said Aury, decidedly upset. 'I don't think we have time to—'

'Aury,' Moriana said gently, 'don't worry about it. We don't have anything that fits this dress. You know it as well as I do. There's no shame in it. Besides, I have it on good authority that I'm intimidating enough, even without the jewels.'

'Well, this is true,' said Aury, slightly mollified.

'Liesendaach has Crown Jewels to match the gown,' said Letitia and promptly blushed. 'It was my job to know what jewels were available to the late Queen. I often designed dresses around them. I wasn't only a seamstress.' The Honourable Letitia looked to Aury. 'What the Lady Aury is to you—that was my role.'

Confidante. Friend. Moriana vowed, then and there, to make this woman an integral part of her world, should she ever reside here permanently. Gifts like Letitia should never be shelved.

'You could always ask His Majesty for access to Liesendaach's jewellery vault,' said Aury boldly. 'Nothing ventured.'

'I could.' Moriana chewed on her lower lip. On the other hand, she'd already been imposing her will all over the place and it seemed somewhat presumptuous to be calling on Liesendaach's treasures. 'Okay, calling for a vote from all present, and no exceptions, Henry, or your mother will find out. Do I ask Theo to let me at Liesendaach's Crown Jewels? If yes, say aye.'

'Aye,' said Aury swiftly, still holding up the amber and ivory beaded gown as her gaze drifted to some point behind Moriana. 'Oh, hello, Your Majesty.'

'Lady Aury,' said a dry voice from the doorway, and

there stood Theo. He wasn't dressed for dinner yet, but he was wearing a suit nonetheless and it fitted him to perfection. 'What do you need?'

'Rubies,' said Aury.

At the same time Letitia said, 'The South Sea Collection.'

'Both,' said Aury, ever the opportunist.

Moriana turned. Theo smiled.

'Your brother is wanting three hundred of my mounted guards to be put at your disposal for a month should you ever decide to marry me, and I said yes,' he said by way of hello. 'Do you seriously think I'll object to you requesting old jewellery that's there for the wearing? One of these actions involves prostrating myself before my cavalry and begging their forgiveness. The other involves walking down to the vault and opening a drawer.'

'I adore pragmatic kings,' said Aury. 'Truly, they're in a league of their own.'

Moriana agreed but she had other angles to pursue. There was a lot to unpack in his offhand comment. 'What do I want three hundred of your mounted guards for?'

'Your wedding procession. Apparently.'

'You've spoken to Augustus?' He must have done. 'Did you know that royal Arunian dowries used to be delivered on the backs of elephants?'

'So I've heard.'

Moriana smiled. Aury looked utterly angelic, as was her wont. Letitia looked vaguely interested, in a serene, grandmotherly fashion that belied her sharp mind, and the guards at the door never moved a muscle—facial muscles included.

'Elephants in procession,' she murmured. 'Think about it. There are lesser evils.'

'Whatever you want from Liesendaach's vaults by way of jewellery you can have,' he countered. 'Anything rubies and the South Sea Collection. What else?'

'That's it.'

Letitia nodded. Aury nodded. Henry observed.

'I'm cultivating a new image that involves less austerity and more…something,' Moriana explained.

'*Something* being a whole lot more in-your-face fairy tale beauty,' added Aury.

'I can't wait.'

Hopefully he could. 'Is there a battle room where we gather beforehand to discuss strategy?'

'Not until now,' Theo murmured. 'But stateroom six should serve the purpose. Anything else you need?'

'The name of every person in attendance tonight that you've ever been intimate with.' The words were out of her mouth before she could call them back.

Theo looked as calm as ever, even if it felt as if everyone else in the room had taken a breath and held it.

'That's not a list you need to worry about,' he said.

His opinion, not hers. Forewarned was forearmed. 'Shall I simply assume everyone between twenty and fifty is a possibility, then?'

'You can assume it won't be a problem.' His voice carried a cool warning. 'Leave us,' he told everyone else in the room, and they left and Moriana held his gaze defiantly. She shouldn't have asked for the list in front of his people or hers. Chances were she shouldn't have asked for it at all, but she wanted to be as prepared as she could for the evening ahead, and that included being prepared for smiling barbs from the women Theo had bedded and then spurned.

He strode lazily over to where she sat at her dressing table and took up the space Aury usually occupied, facing her and a little to the right.

'Want to tell me what's wrong?' he asked quietly.

'Nerves.' Enough to make her hands shake when they weren't folded in her lap. Enough to make her drop her gaze. New court, new people, new...*hope* that this thing between her and Theo was going to work out fine. 'Fear of making mistakes tonight. Fear of letting people down.'

'You won't.'

'I just did, when I asked for the list in front of everyone. But I'm not jealous, not...really. I always do this. I like to be prepared.' She gestured towards the sheaf of papers on the dressing table in front of her. It had the name and head shot of every person attending the dinner on it, along with a brief rundown on their interests, family lives and political affiliations.

He picked it up and scanned the first page and the next.

'I have it almost memorised. A couple more hours should do it.'

'You do this for every event you attend?' His eyes were sharp, his expression non-committal.

'I used to.' Her mother had insisted. 'I don't need to be quite as diligent at home any more. I remember them all. I haven't made a mistake in years. I don't want to make mistakes here either.'

He frowned. 'I don't expect you to remember the name and occupation of everyone at dinner tonight. There will be over two hundred people there. No one expects that of you.'

'Which will make it all the better when I do.'

'Are you having fun?' he asked abruptly.

'What?'

'Is this fun for you?'

Not exactly. She'd woken up feeling anxious, had barely touched her breakfast, been blissfully distracted by Theo's daily lesson, and then had reverted straight back to a state of anxiety the moment he'd left.

She had work to do. She still did. 'I don't understand,' she said, and wanted to squirm beneath his fiercely intent gaze. 'It doesn't have to be fun. This is my job. This is what I do.'

'Not today,' he said. 'I have to look at yearling horses this morning. My horse-breeding specialist has brought them in for selection. You can come too. Help us choose.'

'Theo, I don't have time for this.' She put out her hand and he took it, but only to pull her from the chair and coax her to lean into him.

'Humour me.' He could make her melt when his voice was pitched just so. 'I'll have you back in time to dress.'

Which was how she found herself far from the castle, on the other side of the forest, driving alongside a high stone wall that seemed to stretch for miles. Theo drove them through an elaborate set of wrought iron gates and finally the stables came into view.

It was a huge three-sided structure with an arena in the middle as big as a soccer field. She'd seen similar in Arun—where the mounted regiments were based— but never had she seen climbing roses frame the stable stalls the way they did here.

Theo raised his hand in greeting to a woman on the other side of the arena. The woman lifted her hand in return and started walking towards them, and the closer she got the more familiar she seemed.

She had a perfect face and eyes so deeply violet

they looked painted, and she was dressed for riding. The woman was from Moriana's mother's era, and she greeted Theo like an old beloved friend.

'Belle,' he said, 'this is Moriana. Belle is in charge of the horse breeding programme that supplies Liesend-aach's mounted guard.'

The name clued Moriana in, even though she'd never met Belle in person. This was Theo's father's legendary mistress—the circus performer he'd always kept close, no matter what.

'Ah. You know my name.' Belle's smile turned wry. 'Many don't in this day and age but I had a feeling you might. I like to think I was the late King's favourite mistress, but he never did say and I never did ask. And you, of course, are the Arunian Princess. I remember a very young Theo getting positively indignant about you from time to time. Apparently your mother never taught you how to handle boys of his ilk. Trust me, a smile and a compliment would have made him your slave.'

'I would have liked to know that,' Moriana said.

'It's never too late. Come, let me show you the year-lings before I let them out into the arena. Benedict has already been by to make his choices.'

Theo eyed the older woman sharply. 'They're not his choices to make.'

'And yet I value his opinion and so should you,' Belle admonished. 'No one has a better eye for temperament than your cousin—not even you.'

'So tell me what else you look for in the yearlings you choose?' asked Moriana hurriedly, hoping to prevent argument.

'Let me show you instead,' said Belle, gesturing them towards the nearest stall.

It wasn't difficult to feign interest in the horses on

show. They were big grey warmbloods with hundreds of years' worth of breeding behind them, many of them destined to serve in Theo's mounted regiment. There was a gelding with one white leg and Belle hurriedly went on to explain that, aside from colour, the horse had perfect form and his leadership qualities amongst the other yearlings were well established. The horse was unshakeable, Belle said. 'He does everything in his power to compensate for not being the perfect colour.'

'You know we don't take marked horses.'

'Make an exception,' Belle said, but Theo did not reply.

'If you don't keep him, I will,' Belle said next. 'Or Benedict will. He has a soft spot for imperfection, that boy. Here he is now.' She looked beyond them and Moriana turned too, just in time to see Benedict leading a saddled black horse in through the double doors at one end of the stable complex. 'That's Satan,' said Belle. 'I brought his grandsire with me when I left the circus, and he's a menace to ride. Too smart for his own good. Benedict always takes him out when he visits. I get the impression they both enjoy the challenge.'

Benedict had seen them and nodded in their direction. Theo's expression hardened.

'He won't come to you, if that's what you're worried about,' said Belle drily. 'Even as a boy he knew better than to abandon a freshly ridden horse in my stables.'

True enough, Benedict handed the saddle off to a groom and haltered the horse himself before leading it to the wash area. But he looked back at Theo and beckoned him over with the tiniest tilt of his head.

'Have you asked after his father yet today?'

'The physicians keep me updated.'

'Physicians don't know politics,' said Belle. 'Perhaps you should see what he wants.'

'Did he know I was going to be here?'

'He's here every morning, Theodosius, from around five a.m. onwards, and I put him to work. Just like when he was a boy.'

With a curt, 'Excuse me,' Theo headed towards his cousin.

'Shall we continue our rounds?' Belle asked Moriana and, without waiting for a reply, made her way to the next stall. This one was a filly, proud and fully grey.

'I've never seen Theo so easily led,' Moriana said finally, polite conversation be damned. 'How did you do that?'

'It helps that I've known both those boys since their teens. They were inseparable once.'

'Do you know why that changed?'

'I have my suspicions.'

'A woman?'

Belle snorted. 'They never fought over women—there were always so many to choose from—and for Benedict, men and women both. No. I fear the rift was caused by something far less mundane.'

'Can it be mended?'

'I try to help.' Belle smiled. 'Perhaps you will try too. Now, *this* filly has an interesting bloodline...'

Theo didn't wait until Benedict had finished hosing down the horse before speaking. *Get in, get out, keep it short.* Those were his rules when dealing with Benedict. 'You have something to say?'

Benedict nodded, not even sparing him a glance as he turned the hose off and picked up a nearby scraper. 'You're not going to like it.'

No surprises there.

'My father filed the petition for your dismissal early this morning. He says he has the numbers and he doesn't care that I've no intention of challenging you for the position and that there is no other option from our bloodline. He's simply in it for the chaos now. It's his parting gift to you.'

'He has to know I'll fight it.'

'I'm sure he does.'

'And that I'll win.'

'You usually do.' Benedict began stripping water from the horse's back. He rode them hard, as a rule, but never beyond what a horse would willingly take and the care he took of his ride afterwards would have done an Olympic athlete proud. 'You could announce your engagement to Moriana and bury the petition within a day.'

He could. That had been his intention all along and he'd made no secret of it. And yet... *Moriana First.* 'Not happening,' he grated.

'Why not? It's the perfect solution. You've always been hard for her.'

'Because I've already asked and she didn't accept.'

Wicked amusement danced across Benedict's face. '*You* couldn't get the girl? Oh, that's beautiful.'

Never give Benedict ammunition. Why could Theo never remember that? 'If I applied pressure to Moriana now and appealed to her sense of duty and the need for ongoing regional stability, I *would* get the girl. But I'm not going to do it. For the first time in her life Moriana has a chance to make up her own mind about what she wants to do and who she wants to be, going forward. I'm not going to take that away from her.'

'You're getting soft.'

It wasn't a compliment. 'You want to know what Moriana was up in her rooms doing just now? She was memorising tonight's guest list. She has dossiers of information on every guest invited. And she was miserable. Near frantic with worry that she wouldn't perform to expectations. That's not the life I want for her. She deserves more. She has to believe she can find happiness here, and I'll wait on her answer for eternity if I have to. I will not put time pressure on this decision. My court, my people, they can all *wait* on her answer.'

'And if her answer is no?'

Benedict sounded strangely subdued and now Theo was the one who needed to be doing something with his hands. He picked up a towel and began to rub the horse dry. 'If it's no, only then will I consider other options. Because she's it for me.' It was easier to say it to the side of a horse than it was to say it to a person. 'She always has been.'

Voices carried here. Belle had to know it, for she'd shepherded Moriana into a stall to examine a foaling mare. They were out of sight but plenty close enough to overhear the conversation between Theo and Benedict. And now the older woman was leaning against a stable wall, scuffing patterns in the sawdust with her boot, listening, as Moriana was listening, and Theo was putting his crown on the line. Declaring his allegiance not to his country first but to Moriana's happiness.

And then Belle's gaze met hers. 'I've only ever loved one man,' Belle said quietly. 'I gave up my world for him and I loved him as hard as I could—whenever he wanted, wherever he wanted—and he took, and he took, and he *took*. I've always told myself a King can never afford to put a woman first, but he can. And some do.'

And then Belle moved forward and her hand snaked

out to catch a tiny hoof that had appeared beneath the mare's tail. 'Aha. This foal is breech. I thought as much.' She smiled conspiratorially. 'Do you want to see what those two boys can do when they work together?' And in a louder voice that was bound to carry, 'Theo! Benedict! We need a hand. Or two.'

CHAPTER NINE

MORIANA DRESSED FOR the evening with uncommon care. Some of Liesendaach's Crown Jewels had been delivered to her room in her absence, and Aury and Letitia fussed and compared and had a glorious time and Moriana let them. The list of names she hadn't finished memorising sat to one side of her dressing table. A little wooden box sat on the other side, and she knew exactly what was in it, even if Aury didn't. She'd put it there herself as a reminder of a decision that needed to be made. A decision Theo had not asked her to revisit but he *needed* her to revisit it nonetheless.

She thought he might have said something about the petition on their way back from the stables, but he hadn't. He'd talked of the new foal instead—a little colt that he and Benedict had delivered with ease.

When they reached the palace entrance he'd excused himself from her company. He had a little business to attend to before the dinner, he'd said. And kept her clueless as to the nature of it.

The amber gown with the beaded bodice won them all over once she had it on, and the diamonds and pearls of the South Sea Collection complemented it beautifully. First the earrings and then the necklace. There was a bracelet too, but she waved it away. 'I think the white gloves instead,' she said. The ones that went up and over her elbows. She could take them off at some point. And then…

She reached for the little wooden box and snapped it open, her decision made.

And then Theo would have his answer.

She slid it onto her wedding ring finger and Aury gasped. 'Is that…?'

'Yes.'

'Congratulations, Your Highness,' said Letitia.

'When did this *happen*?' asked Aury.

'He asked me before we came here. I've been trying to decide what to do ever since. And now I have.'

'But…are you sure?' Aury's eyes were dark with concern. 'I mean, I know the two of you get on better than you used to, but if you're going to obsess over all of his past conquests, I mean, that's not a habit you want to get into if you want to stay healthy.'

'I know,' she murmured. 'I'm over it.' *She's it for me. She always has been. She has to believe she can find happiness here.*

The sex, the fun, all the attention Theo had paid to her needs these past few days had come together in one blinding moment of clarity. He cared for her. He was willing to put her needs before the needs of the Crown and his own best interests.

Theo might not call that love, but it was close enough.

She wanted this.

She wanted him.

Duty and passion—and a little bit of trust and that thing they weren't calling *love*—had made the decision easy. She *wanted* to stand beside this man, proudly and for ever.

And love him.

'Wish me luck,' she said as she pulled the glove on over the ring and began to work her fingers into it. 'He doesn't know my answer yet.'

Aury snorted. 'You're going to slay him.'

'One can only hope.' She worked the other glove on, took a deep breath and reached for the royal blue sash that proclaimed her a Princess of Arun. Aury helped her slip it on and fastened it with a clasp that proclaimed the highest honours a King could bestow. When she straightened again her posture was perfect.

'You will not fail me,' she told the regal woman staring back at her from the mirror. 'You are a Princess of Arun and a future Queen of Liesendaach. You've got this.'

Aury nodded, her expression grave. The lady-in-waiting had heard it all before, the pep talks that masked Moriana's screaming insecurity every time she had to perform in public.

'Milady, Your Highness—' Letitia looked to the floor, her fingers twisting together with either hesitation or anxiety '—on behalf of myself and…and others—all the people you've taken the time to get to know this week, so many of whose names you already know—we are so very proud to serve you. We are grateful for your care.' She raised her eyes. 'We will not fail you either.'

She never forgot a name. Theo watched in outright awe as Moriana worked the room. He'd seen her in action before but that was on her turf, with dignitaries she'd grown up with. That she could so easily converse here was a testament to ruthless discipline and hours of preparation.

She favoured no one, except perhaps Benedict, who

she'd shared a few words with towards the beginning of the evening.

Theo's uncle was unwell, unable to make the dinner and receiving no visitors. Theo had already uttered that line more times than he cared to remember. He wondered cynically if he hadn't been playing into his uncle's hands by not allowing him visitors. Would so many from his court support the petition to dethrone Theo if they knew Constantine of Liesendaach was dying?

They must know, some of them. And they were behind the petition regardless.

Theo had been in a foul mood ever since his conversation with Benedict and not even saving the little colt had shifted it. Did his court really want him gone or were they simply trying to mobilise him towards marriage? He knew what they wanted.

He'd never thought dragging his feet on the issue could cost him the Crown.

He'd put a security detail on Benedict the minute he'd returned to the palace. He wanted to know who Benedict spoke to, who he phoned, what was said.

Benedict hadn't gone to see his father before dinner. He'd called the Cordova house and spoken to the brother, a curt conversation that hadn't gone well, according to the security team. He'd dressed for dinner. Taken two whiskies and paced his sitting room until it was time to attend.

Theo wished he knew how to trust his cousin the way he'd trusted him as a child.

Had Benedict been complicit in his father's plans?

If only he *knew.*

Theo watched his cousin move assuredly between one group of people and the next, and wondered exactly when the thought had taken hold that Benedict had to have known about his father's plans.

Shortly after Theo had obtained proof of his uncle's actions, he figured grimly. He'd re-examined every move the people around him had ever made, and Benedict hadn't made the cut.

Moriana and her brother had, and so had Casimir. Valentine and his sister—the royal children of Thallasia—had made the grade. No one older had—there'd been too much doubt.

'What's he done?' asked a voice from beside him, and there stood Theo's Head of Household Staff, a picture of elegance and efficiency in black trousers, black shirt and buttoned blazer.

'Who?'

Sam sent him one of those looks that told him she was aware of his avoidance tactic but she didn't call him on it outright.

'Why are you here?' She usually left the running of state dinners to the functions team.

'Her Highness wanted things done a certain way tonight. I'm making sure it happens.' Sam looked unruffled.

Theo eyed her warily. 'Is that a problem?' he asked.

'No problem. Quite frankly, it's an honour. This is me wanting to make a good impression on a woman who can teach me, and possibly everyone else around here, how best to run a royal household.'

He nodded, his attention already returning to his cousin. Moriana was with Benedict again; she'd sought him out and the conversation they were having looked to be a private one, their dark heads bent towards one another, familiar enough to be close in each other's space. Any closer and tomorrow's press would have them eloping.

The press was fascinated by the newly emerging Moriana—the one who'd always moved through the spotlight with seeming effortlessness. Her dress made her look every inch the Princess she was and the Liesendaach jewels had not gone unnoticed. Her long white gloves were driving him mad. All he wanted to do was take her some place private and peel them off, and why stop there?

Theo watched as Benedict smiled unhappily and Moriana touched her hand to his forearm in comfort as she started to speak again.

And then she pulled back and began to peel her gloves off. Why the hell was she doing that? So she could touch Benedict with her bare hands?

Theo's feet were moving before his brain had even made sense of it. All he knew was that the time for watching from afar was over and that Benedict needed to step away from Moriana right about *now*.

They looked up as he approached, Benedict's gaze widening and then turning assessing.

And then Theo looked down at Moriana's bare arms and hands. Only they weren't quite bare because she was wearing his engagement ring.

Happiness licked through him, fierce and complete. Moriana was his. *To have and to hold*, and he'd never wanted anything more than he wanted this. His world narrowed to a point, sharp and bright, as he lifted her hand and put the ring to his lips, and then his lips to hers. 'Are you sure?' he asked, rough and gruff against her lips.

'I'm sure,' she whispered, and put her beringed hand to his cheek. 'I want this.'

'For yourself.' He had to be sure.

'You're very persuasive.'

'Can someone please spare me?' said Benedict. 'I don't want to be sick. The stains, they never come out of the sashes.'

Moriana blushed and dropped her hand. Theo glared at Benedict. 'I'm sorry—are we boring you?'

'Yes,' said Benedict. 'A thousand times *yes*.'

Never give Benedict a tree branch to club you with. Because he would.

'Benedict, there you are!'

Theo turned to scowl at whoever dared interrupt them and there stood Angelique Cordova, wearing a red gown and a serene smile. *Perfect.* That was all they needed. But she was Benedict's date, and Benedict stepped back to allow more room in the circle for her.

'I gather you got Enrique's message?' Angelique said next.

'Yes.' Benedict smiled bleakly, but then he rallied and gave her a kiss on the cheek. 'Thank you for coming.'

'Someone had to support you, darling. We couldn't *all* leave you hanging. We're family.'

'How so?' asked Theo.

'Family of the heart,' she said next. 'Bear with my brother, Benedict. He's frightened for you as well as himself. He thinks now is not the time and I happen to agree with him.' She glanced up, as if only now noticing Moriana, and dropped into an elegant curtsey.

Benedict sighed, and waved his hand in a languid parody of an introduction. 'Your Highness, Princess Moriana of Arun, and so on and so forth, may I present my lovely companion for this evening, the utterly fearless Angelique Cordova, one of the brightest lights of my life. Or, at the very least, a matchstick in the darkness.'

'Pig,' she said and turned towards Moriana and curt-seyed again. 'A pleasure to meet you, Your Highness. I've heard so much about you.'

'Tell her you have so much in common,' Benedict prompted his date maliciously.

'Be a boor then,' Angelique replied smoothly. 'I intend to do no such thing.'

'I'm happy to finally meet you, Ms Cordova.' Moriana had rallied in the face of the interruption and was every inch the regal princess. 'I hear we have a lot in common.'

Theo blinked. Benedict crowed a laugh. Angelique looked momentarily startled but recovered quickly.

'Only in that I gave the world countless opportunities to tease Theo for his utter inability to tell two women apart. Of course, that then backfired because men will be men, and I'm now known as a woman not memorable enough to require close attention. I truly wish we'd never pulled that foolish stunt, but the world still turns, no?'

'Indeed it does,' Moriana murmured.

'May I offer my congratulations on your engagement?' the woman said next.

'You're the first to congratulate us,' said Moriana lightly. 'Thank you.'

'Please, let me be the second to offer my congratulations,' said Benedict. 'Assuming, of course, that Theo doesn't mess it up by assuming you don't really mean it.'

'But I do really mean it,' said Moriana.

'Good for you. Tell him often.'

And then Sam was between them, drawing Theo's attention with a glance. 'Your Majesty, my apology for interrupting but your uncle's physicians are requesting a word with both you and Prince Benedict. Now.'

That couldn't be good. 'Where are they?'

'In your uncle's room, Your Majesty.'

'Go,' said Moriana. 'I can hold the fort here until your return. I suspect Ms Cordova and I can amuse ourselves and doubtless find more shared interests in your absence.'

The mind boggled. Theo wanted not to think about it. Ever.

'Yes, that's not going to set tongues wagging at all,' murmured Angelique Cordova, heavy on the caution. 'Are you sure?'

'I don't think tomorrow is going to be a slow news day,' Moriana said and pressed a kiss first to Theo's cheek before turning to Benedict and doing the same. 'Go.'

'Scary woman,' said Benedict when they were halfway along the west wing corridor. There were guards to the rear and more up ahead but otherwise they were alone.

'Which one?'

'Yours. I waver between being totally intimidated by her one minute and wanting to bask in her attention the next.'

'Stay away from her.' Of all the emotions seething inside him, this one was foremost.

Benedict frowned and glanced Theo's way. 'I'm not a threat to you where she's concerned.'

'I know better than to believe you.'

'Then you're a fool.'

Benedict subsided into silence and Theo was glad of it. They walked the rest of the wing in silence until they reached the suite of rooms that currently housed Benedict's father. Two security guards stood sentry; one of them opened the door for them and Theo stood back to let Benedict through first—and that *was* a first. Benedict's startled glance and hesitation in stepping forward confirmed it.

'He's not my dying father,' Theo said and waved his cousin forward. It was a callous move rather than an act of respect and Benedict knew it.

'You're a monster,' Benedict muttered.

An insecure, needy, untrusting one, yes.

Theo let Benedict ask most of the questions as they spoke first to the physicians and then entered the bedroom where Constantine of Liesendaach lay. They'd taken away all life support machinery and the man lay in bed, his eyes closed and the shallow rise and fall of his chest the only indication that he still lived. *Not long now*, the physicians had said. *Tonight.* The shadow of death was in the room.

Benedict sat beside his father and took his hand, but when the old man's eyes slitted open they focused on Theo, not Benedict.

'I knew you'd come,' said Constantine, his voice no more than a rasping protest against a throat too close to seizing. 'You want to confront me before I die.'

'Maybe I do. Maybe it's time.' Theo had kept the knowledge so close that sometimes he'd felt as if it was strangling him. But it was family business and if Constantine wanted to air it, family would bear witness. 'I know you killed my family,' he told the dying man. 'I've had proof of it for years and I don't care for your denial and I sure as hell don't care to hear your confession. You did it. I know it. I know why, and I only have one question left. Did Benedict know of your plans?'

The cadaverous old man wet his shrunken lips with his tongue, tried to speak and then started to laugh before any words formed. 'That keep you awake…at night…boy?'

'Yes.' It was no lie, and there was no ignoring Benedict's pale and frozen face.

'Father, what—?'

Benedict stopped speaking when his father started coughing but it wasn't so much coughing as it was cracked and rattling laughter. 'My weak, pathetic…son. Think I don't know…about your sodomy…or your plans to renounce your family? No loss. No loss.'

Benedict recoiled from that serpent's tongue but Theo moved in; his need to know the truth was riding him hard. 'I'm talking to you, old man. Did Benedict know of your plans?'

'Weak…like his mother. Soft…'

'Answer me!'

His uncle's eyes gleamed with pure malice. 'Don't think I…will.'

But Theo wasn't looking at his uncle any more; his attention was solely for his cousin and the blank, uncomprehending shock in Benedict's eyes as he stared at Theo. Theo pushed away from his chair, toppling it as he stood.

'Did you know? Is that why you saved me?' This time Theo's question was for Benedict.

'Is that what you think? You truly believe me capable of saving you and letting the rest of your family fall? What for, Theo? To what purpose? Because I'm my father's son? Does it sound to you as if I enjoy his approval?' Benedict looked shattered, lost in memories maybe, or mired in his father's cruel contempt. '*This* is what you've been punishing me for all these years?'

Benedict stepped back, and then again, still facing them both. As if he didn't dare turn his back on either of them. And then he drew himself up. 'Father, I've never been the son you wanted. I've always known it. I used to crave your approval, more than anything. I don't any more. I have value—maybe not to you or to the King, but to some, and I am content.' Benedict turned to Theo next. 'I renounce you.' Benedict's voice shook. 'I absolve you of all dealings with me, going forward. We are not kin. I have no King. Now, get out of my sight while my father dies, and then I will get out of yours.'

It was no small matter, renouncing one's family. It was a testament to how badly Theo had handled things here tonight. He'd left cool intellect at the door, already emotionally engaged and disinclined to give Benedict the benefit of the doubt. He'd let the old man get to him while simultaneously trying to analyse Benedict's reaction, and now the old man was laughing, and Benedict was broken and Theo was responsible. 'Do you need—would you like anyone else with you? I can bring Angelique.'

'Unfortunately, she's not the Cordova for me.' Benedict crossed to the sideboard and poured a full tumbler of Scotch.

'Her brother then. I can get him here.'

'Why? So you can display your tolerance for our kind?'

'So you're not alone,' Theo said doggedly.

'Too late.' Benedict scowled. 'He won't come.'

'Then I'll stay.' He held his cousin's bitter gaze.

'You just want to hear your family's murderer draw his last breath.'

'I would see that chapter of my life closed and a new one opened, yes,' Theo admitted. 'Benedict, I'm sorry I ever doubted you.'

'Yeah, well.' Benedict drained his drink in one hit and opted to pour another. 'Your loss.'

Constantine of Liesendaach, former Prince Regent and father to Benedict, died during the main course of Moriana's first State Dinner in Liesendaach. Both Theo and Benedict were absent when the meal was served and rumours had already started to spread as to why. Some said they were in conflict over Moriana's favouring of Benedict earlier in the evening. Others declared Angelique Cordova the bone over which they fought. Moriana withstood the mutterings until the main course had been cleared away and then stood and held up her hand for silence.

Two hundred people quietened and stared at her with varying degrees of tolerance. Her introduction to Liesendaach society wasn't exactly going to plan but there was nothing she could do except stand tall and bear their regard.

She was a Princess of Arun and the future Queen of Liesendaach, assuming Theo didn't want his ring back. And she would damn well command their attention if she wanted it.

'Many of you here tonight have offered congratulations on my engagement to your King, and I welcome it,' she said. 'All of you are no doubt wondering where my fiancé is right now. You might be thinking what could possibly lure him from my side? Is Moriana of Arun being jilted? *Again.*'

A titter of nervous laughter ran the length of the room.

'Exactly,' she said drily, and lowered her hand now that she had their attention. 'Former Prince Regent, Constantine of Liesendaach, died ten minutes ago. Prince Benedict and the King attended him, and won't be returning to dine with you this evening. Dessert will be served directly, after which we'll bring the evening to an early conclusion. I look forward to meeting you all again under easier circumstances and I thank you for your understanding.'

She didn't expect applause and she didn't get it. Her appetite for sweets was non-existent. For the first time in her life, she walked out of a function and didn't care if she was doing right or wrong. She caught the Cordova twin's eye on the way to the door and gestured for her to join her. Benedict had brought her here. Moriana would not abandon her.

'What now?' asked the other woman once they were clear of the dining room. But Moriana's confidence had run out.

'We go and find them.' Although, given the way tonight was running, they'd probably stumble straight into whatever it was that Benedict and Theo needed to sort out between themselves.

'I need to call my brother,' said the other woman. 'He'll want to know.'

'Brothers are like that.' Augustus too could do with an update. 'Do you need privacy? I'm sure there are rooms available.'

'Here is fine, Your Highness.'

She could like Angelique Cordova, given the chance. 'See if you can get your brother here. I'll see to it that he has security clearance.'

'I'll try, Your Highness, but, with all due respect, it may be better if I simply find Benedict and take him home. My brother will be waiting.'

Moriana nodded and turned to walk away.

'Your Highness, thank you for your patronage this evening. It was more than I expected.'

It was more than Moriana had expected to give the Cordova twin, truth be told, but she didn't regret it. 'My mother used to tell me to face my fears rather than let them grow. And I did fear you, just a little, as a woman who might have held Theo's heart.'

Angelique Cordova smiled ruefully. 'I never even came close, and neither did my sister.'

'Tell your sister I'd like to meet her too. Perhaps we could all go riding one day. Tell me, do you ride?'

'Since infancy, Your Highness. My father breeds horses in Spain. They're quite famous.' Angelique Cordova paused. 'But then, you already knew that.'

'I did. Still. There's a forest here I've yet to explore and an entire regiment of mounted guards with nothing to do but tend horses. I'm sure some of them could be persuaded to accompany us.'

'That would definitely be a pretty ride.'

Aury was going to like this woman too.

Angelique Cordova took her leave, pulling a phone from her evening bag and retreating to the far corner of the ballroom foyer for privacy.

As for finding Theo and Benedict, Sam was heading her way and would probably know. 'Where are they?'

'Benedict went to his rooms and the King is in the Lower West Library. Past the Rafael, two doors down on the left. Neither of them are in fine spirits.'

That was hardly a surprise. 'You'll see to it that the guests take their leave?'

'Leave it with us.'

'Thank you, Sam. The meal was delicious and the service was prompt and unobtrusive. Let the kitchen know I'm pleased.'

'Yes, ma'am.'

'And have some food sent to Theo. He hasn't eaten yet.'

'Yes, ma'am. Shall I organise a meal for the Prince as well?'

'No. Just take Angelique Cordova to him once she finishes her call.'

Moriana found Theo in a room that reminded her less of a library and more of her father's den. Dark leather and wood dominated a setting scattered with low reading lamps, deep wingback chairs and a wall full of books with ancient spines. There was a bottle of whisky on the table at Theo's side and one crystal tumbler. He watched her come in but said nothing. He didn't smile.

'I'm guessing it was a rough finish,' she said, approaching cautiously. She didn't know this Theo, the one with the burning eyes and the coiled tension. Her teasing suitor was gone and in his place stood a man with a gleam in his eye that said, *Don't push me—stay back.*

She never had learned how to back away from a situation she didn't know how to deal with. She'd only ever learned how to push on and muddle through.

Theo didn't answer her so she filled his silence with words. 'The dinner is winding up. I announced that your uncle had died and you wouldn't be returning. I hope I didn't overstep.'

'Do you ever? You're the perfect princess. What more could a man want?'

Something else, judging by the sneer on his face, and she should have retreated then and there and left him to his grieving. The ring on her finger had never felt heavier. She hadn't even *warned* him she would be wearing it. 'May I stay and have a drink with you?' she asked.

'Help yourself.'

She did and eyed him pensively while she sipped. 'Did you and Benedict clear up your differences?'

'No.' Theo drained the rest of his drink.

'Is it because Liesendaach's royal family can't accommodate his relationship preferences?'

'Benedict can bed whoever he wants.' Theo's lips curled. 'As long as it's not you.'

'Where did *that* come from? You know I will never encourage Benedict to see me as romantically available. I mean…how can you not know that? I'm wearing your ring. What have I *ever* done to make you or anyone else think I'll not honour my promises?'

'Nothing.' He put his drink down and slumped forward in his chair, elbows to knees and hands clasped loosely together. He fingered the royal signet ring on his middle finger, looking for all the world like a penitent boy. 'I trust you. I do. I was just…jealous earlier, when you put your hand on his arm.'

'It was an act of comfort. His partner refused to attend the dinner. He was upset.'

'He was playing you.'

'No, Theo. He wasn't. Benedict is at his most vicious when he's upset. How can you not know that? It's all he ever is around you. And as for you… You never give him the benefit of the doubt. Why is that? What did he do to you?'

Theo ducked his head and ran his hand through his hair. 'Trust, right? I need to trust you with my secrets and my failings, even the worst of them. Even the ones you'll think less of me for. Especially them. For years I've held Benedict partly responsible for something he knew nothing about. I should have trusted him. I didn't.'

Trust wasn't his strong suit. He knew it. Everyone knew it.

'You could ask for your cousin's forgiveness,' she suggested.

Theo snorted. 'Yeah, that'll fix it.'

'It might.'

'You know *nothing*, Moriana! Why are we even talking about this?'

'Because you're upset and I want to help you!' Her temper rose to match his. 'It may have escaped your notice but it hasn't escaped mine that I still don't know what the hell you're talking about. Why do you limit yourself and not share a problem? Why do you limit *me*?'

'You're not limited!' *Here* was the fiery boy she remembered from childhood. The one who fought and scrapped and roared. 'Whatever you want to do, *you do*. My palace is open to you for reorganisation, my regiments mobilised at your request, education and health reports sit on your desk. Every time you want me to put my hands on you, *I do*. There is nothing I wouldn't do for you!'

'Except confide in me.'

'*I do confide in you*. I just did! The details are irrelevant. My uncle is dead and I will not grieve for him. Benedict is gone, and I don't blame him and I can't fix it. Enough! I bend for you, I do. Come on, Moriana, *please*. You need to bend too.'

She looked away rather than continuing to burn beneath the fierceness of his gaze. His cousin was gone, his uncle was dead and she was making things worse.

'I'm sorry; you're right. I came in here to see if there was anything you needed me to do. I didn't come here to push or to argue with you, and you never asked for my company in the first place, and I have no experience with grief other than when my mother passed and I remember when you made me sit at her funeral and gave me a glass of water and it was just what I needed and right now I want to give you just what you need and I'm not, and I'm sorry, and I'm babbling and I need to stop right now and leave you be.' She dug her nails into her palm and tried to find her lost composure. It was definitely time for her to leave. 'I apologise. I'll try to do better next time.'

She set her glass down and headed for the door, her back ramrod-straight and her heart thundering. She'd screwed up. Talked too much. Made things worse, not better. *Stop, Moriana. Don't panic. Breathe.*

He hadn't made her take the damn ring off. Not yet, at any rate.

She had her hand on the brass doorknob and another breath of air in her lungs when his palm snaked out to slam against the door and keep it shut. She hadn't heard him move, she'd been too busy berating herself, but she felt his arms come around her and saw his other hand land on the other side of the door, trapping her between his big body and smooth oak.

'Stay.' His breath warmed her cheek. 'Please. I know I'm not good company, just… I don't want to be alone.'

It wasn't the same as *I want you to stay because you're the only one for me* but she stilled her hand on the doorknob nonetheless. *Stay. Concentrate on the request and leave his reasoning the hell alone.*

'Stay,' he said again, and she closed her eyes as he pressed his lips to her neck. 'Sit with me, read with me, curse me. Just don't leave.'

She pressed her forehead to the door and let her body melt into his. 'I don't want to. I'm trying to be what you need.'

She turned and brought her lips to his, to offer comfort and a way for him to forget, and he took to the kiss like a dying man to water. There was no finesse, no lesson here, only need and heat and Moriana was power-less in the face of it.

He picked her up and carried her to the overstuffed leather daybed, all without releasing her mouth. She ended up stretched out beneath him, her fingers at his collar and tie and then his jacket as she slid it from his shoulders, but her dress stayed on and her jewellery stayed on and her hair stayed up.

She raised her hands to one earring and began to take it off, but he shook his head and clenched his jaw.

'Leave them on.'

'I can't.' She had one earring out before he'd even sat up. 'The jewellery's too valuable to lie on and the gown is heavier than it looks. I want them gone.' She took the other earring out and held them in one hand as she fumbled with the clasp on the necklace. It was too complicated, never meant for the wearer alone to take off, and certainly not in a hurry. 'Please.' She captured his mouth again with hers, soft and crushed where he was hard and demanding. Willing. And he was still will-ing too, was he not? 'I don't want the worry of them.'

She needed him to know that there was a woman be-neath the perfect princess image.

'Turn around.'

'One of my favourite phrases. Who knew?' she said raggedly but she turned around so he could remove the necklace. The zip was to the side of the gown but he found it without prompting and she held her breath as he slid it down her side and over her hip. She let the dress fall to the floor and there was no bra to bother with, only panties and high heeled shoes, and she slipped out of those too, before he could say *leave them on.*

She wanted nakedness and skin on skin and nothing between them but sweat and sweet promises.

'Still every inch a princess,' he offered when she turned around to face him, but he stepped in closer and slid his hand up and around the nape of her neck. 'It's in the curve of your neck.' His hand slid around to the front and his thumb tilted her head until she raised her eyes to his. 'And the tilt of your jaw. It's in your heart.' Fingertips slid back down her throat and over her curves until he flattened his palm just below her breast. 'My heart now.'

Because it was.

Another kiss. A ragged sigh.

He reached for his cufflinks and then for his belt and shortly thereafter he too stood naked and proud, pinning her with his hungry gaze. She was ready for whatever came next. Mindless pleasure and the losing of self. She could help him there.

He drew her down onto the leather daybed, on his back with her half draped over him. He ran his hand from neck to flank and then urged her leg up and over his exquisitely hard body, opening her up but not boxing her in, pressing against her but not pushing in.

'That's it,' he murmured into her mouth but she was through with being schooled by him.

She dragged her lips from his and started again at his shoulder, tasting his skin until she reached his pebbled nipple. She closed her mouth over him and sucked, darkly pleased when his breath left his body with a whoosh and his head dropped back on the bed.

Moriana rubbed her cheek against his skin as his body bowed towards her, releasing the tight little nub in favour of settling herself across him more fully. He let her wriggle until she'd found the most comfortable place to sit, and it was like the rubbing lesson all over again, with her finding friction against the silken hardness of his erection. She looked down towards where they weren't quite joined as intimately as she wanted them to be and swallowed hard at the sight. There was so *much* of him still visible, and how it was *ever* going to fit was still a mystery to her at this point.

She wasn't scared, but she could admit to being ever so slightly daunted.

He'd been over every inch of her body with lips and hands but he'd always pulled back from truly claiming her. She'd thought he was waiting until after the wedding, part of his royal need for legitimate heirs, but now she wondered if he hadn't simply been letting her get used to the idea of something that size going places no man had ever been.

'Are you sure about this?' There was no judgement in his quiet question.

'I want to. You want to forget, right? This is how you do it.'

'I won't forget this,' he said, his eyes darkening. 'We need to get you ready.'

'I'm ready.'

'Not quite. You're still capable of thought.'

Five minutes later, that was no longer a problem. He'd used his fingers to tease and tempt and stretch and a wave of pleasure hovered just out of reach. Skin on skin, one hand soothing as the other inflamed, he murmured nonsense words of encouragement as she took him in hand and lined him up until she felt the wide, wet press of him against her opening. Her gaze met his and his eyelashes fluttered as she gained an inch. She bit her lip, because there was no way this didn't hurt, but he'd never been wrong about pleasure yet and if she could just get *past* this first bit she'd be fine.

She willed herself to relax and gained another inch

that felt like a mile and lost her breath somewhere along the way. No more, surely, except he was less than half-way in and she was stuck. 'I—help?'

He took control, hands that had been quietly strok-ing and coaxing, turning firm as he cupped her buttocks and slid her off him, not all the way but enough that she could breathe.

'Circle your hips.' Big hands guided her way and slickness returned and this time when she slid back down on him she ventured further. This time he helped by drawing back before she did, his palm coming to cover her belly and his thumb gently pressing down on her sensitive flesh. 'Better?'

They were going to be here all night.

'You're thinking again,' he rumbled.

'Patience isn't one of my gifts.'

His eyes warmed. 'I have enough for both of us.'

He pulled out as he rolled her beneath him and slid down her body, proceeding to turn her into a mind-less, writhing wreck again. This time when he rose back up and entered her it was easier. Slowly, inexorably, he worked his way in and somewhere along the way he stopped being so careful and she stopped worrying about pain versus pleasure, because the pleasure was back and it was constant.

She tilted her hips and he groaned and she thought he might have been seated to the hilt, but then he wrapped his hand beneath one of her knees and brought her leg up and thrust, and *now* he was all the way in and it was tight, and breathtakingly good.

For her, at any rate.

It was more intimate than anything she'd ever experi-enced with him. His previous lessons in sexual exploration had been fun, heady and all too often overwhelming. This was soul-stealing.

She would have more of it.

She drew him closer, sipped delicately at his lips and then licked within. He'd never been more beautiful to her than he was at this moment, his tightly controlled movements bound only by his will.

'Please,' she whispered, because surely he needed more than this. His focus had never wavered from his quest to make this good for her, not once. When did he get to let go and feel? 'I'm really, *really* ready.'

His lips quirked above hers. 'What would you have me do?'

'Move.'

The man could follow direction when he wanted to. He raised himself to his knees, still inside her, one hand to her hip and the other to her nub, and he moved. Every stroke sent a tremor through her, every slide and every breath wound her tighter as he coaxed her to a rhythm she somehow already knew. Sensation piled in on her—it was too much, too good, and she wasn't a quiet lover, she discovered, but neither was Theo. The flush on his cheekbones had spread down his neck and across his chest, a sheen of sweat made his skin glow, and there was nothing she wanted more than to see him come undone.

'Tell me what you need.' His voice was hoarse but his eyes spoke true. He meant it.

'Give me all of you.' They were thoughtless words but true. He stilled above her and then with a groan that choked out like a sob he let go of his restraint.

It took him less than half a dozen savage thrusts before she felt her body clamp around him. She tightened unbearably as the rest of her scattered to the four winds.

There was no thought beyond this, and him, and when he followed moments later she could have sworn she could feel him spilling into her, claiming and being claimed in equal measure.

'This. I need this, whatever this is,' she whispered against his shoulder and his arms tightened around her. 'Let me love you.'

CHAPTER TEN

Moriana was silent in the aftermath, but it wasn't the comfortable, sated silence a man could fall asleep in. This silence was prickly, tense, and for the first time in forever Theo wondered if he'd done wrong by a woman sexually. Had he been too reckless, too forceful, too greedy? Or all of those things? Because with Moriana involved all bets were off. Smoothness deserted him and neediness ruled.

Self-control fled when passion crept in.

He could barely believe she was his.

She'd curled into his side, her cheek to his shoulder and her hair a rampant tumble of curls. Her limbs were curled around his and the evidence of their joining lay wet between them both.

'You okay?' he asked gruffly, when what he wanted to ask was, *Was I good enough for you? Do you still want me the way you did before? Have you changed your mind about all this?*

He tightened his arm around her and ran his fingers over the knuckles of the hand she'd placed on his chest, which led him to the ring she wore, the one he'd chosen for his Queen. It was about time he admitted to himself that Moriana had always been there in the back of his mind. Practically perfect. Unobtainable. Already taken.

And claimed now, by him.

He turned, ever so slightly, and pressed a kiss into her hair. 'Have I rendered you speechless?'

'No, just sated. And thinking.'

'Thinking what?'

'That making love to you was more than I ever imagined. And I imagined a lot.'

He could stand to hear a little more. He brushed his fingers over her ring, loving that she'd chosen to wear it. 'When did you decide?'

'Oh.' Her fingers curled into themselves a little but he wasn't having it; he wanted their fingers entwined and now they were. 'Well. Today some time, around about the time you delivered that foal, or a little bit before then. After letting me at the Crown Jewels but before the dinner. And then the petition to remove you because you weren't married got resurrected and I figured—'

'You figured *what*?'

'I figured now would be a good time to tell you I was ready,' she said.

He pulled away. Not hard but enough for him to see her face. Such a beautiful face. The one that now haunted his dreams.

'You knew the petition had landed.'

'I—'

He could see the truth in her eyes.

'I knew,' she said.

'Get up.' True rage had always settled on him cold rather than hot. 'Get dressed. I don't need you to marry me because it's your royal duty to shore up my reign.'

'I'm not.'

'Get up! Get dressed. And *get out*. Do you think I want you to do this because duty compels you to? Moriana the perfect, Moriana the good. For God's sake, for once in your life *do what you want!*'

'I did! I am! And if you can't see that you're blind. I love you, Theo. Wholly and without caveats, but no. You can't have that. I'd get too close.' She picked up his trousers and threw them at him. '*You* get out. You're the one who can't stand being here with me like this. Give you a reason, any reason, to mistrust a person and you're there, filling in the blanks. You did it with Benedict. You're doing it with me. So get out and take your conspiracies with you and leave me alone.'

He got up. He put his trousers on and reached for his shirt. 'Moriana—'

'Get out! You don't *see* what other people want you to see. You couldn't accept love if someone laid it at your feet. Benedict loves you. I love you, but no. You can't see past your own towering mistrust.'

'Moriana, I—'

'Please go.' She picked up her dress. 'I don't want to talk to you right now. Just go. And in the morning I'll go.' He looked at her, just looked at her, and, to his utmost horror, got to see Moriana, perfect Princess of Arun, break wide open.

'For heaven's sake, Theo, get out,' she screamed. *'Can't you see I'm giving you exactly what you want?'*

He got out.

He went back to his rooms and sent Aury to her, and Sam to her, and food to her. Everything he could think of except himself.

And then he too held his head in his hands and broke.

She should have seen it coming. Moriana stood at a window in the Queen's suite and looked out over the grounds below, bathed in soft morning light. She'd showered already this morning, and twice last night, but her body still ached in places it had never ached before, and her feelings kept slipping to the surface, bringing hot tears she couldn't afford to show. She *had* seen this coming— Theo's inability to let her into his life and share his innermost thoughts and feelings. And then she'd gone and fallen deeply in love with him anyway.

She's it for me.

That was the moment she'd lost all caution. But those words weren't the same as *I'll fight my demons for you.* They weren't *I'll never hurt you.* Quite the opposite, in fact.

Moriana stared down at the ring on her finger, tracing it with unsteady fingers, twisting it round and round. She'd take it off soon and leave it sitting on the dresser in its box. Engaged for less than twenty-four hours. A new record for Moriana of Arun. The illustrious members of the press were going to crucify her and she could barely raise the will to care.

Let them.

'Milady, will you be breakfasting with the King this morning or shall I see to it that breakfast is served here?' said a voice from the far corner of the room, and she turned and there stood Aury in the doorway, still sleepy and dressed in her nightgown. Aury, who'd come for Moriana last night and got her back to the Queen's quarters with a minimum amount of fuss, and who'd then firmly shut everyone else out and earned Moriana's undying gratitude.

And then Aury had left too, with a sympathetic smile and eyes sure with the knowledge that some things were best worked through alone.

Breakfast. Right. She'd never felt less hungry but it was the principle of the matter. Hearts got given and sometimes those holding them didn't know how to keep them safe, and the sun still rose.

'I'll be having breakfast here, please, Aury. Just some fruit and coffee.'

'No bacon?' Aury shot her a pleading look. 'Bacon on sourdough, with the heritage tomatoes and mushrooms from the gardens. Not that I'm mourning the impending loss of such bounty. At all.'

'All right, that too. And the yoghurt and the passion-fruit and the black sapote.'

'Oh, *yes*,' said Aury. 'And about that outfit you're wearing… It's perfect. Very sensual. Very confident.'

'Good.' Because she wasn't inclined to take it off. The sundress was another from her never-worn-before collection, bright orange and red silks and chiffons, unapologetically fitted to make the most of her curves, and she'd pulled her hair into an untamed ponytail and secured it with a white silk scarf. 'It's the new me.' Moriana liked being confident in her sensuality, a virgin no more. 'I guess I have Theo to thank for that.'

'Or we could call him an emotionally stunted imbecile and not thank him at all,' offered Aury. 'Just a thought.'

But Moriana shook her head and turned back to the view out of the window and the weak sun on her face. 'Let's not. Theo's taught me a lot this week, and a lot of it was good.' He'd encouraged her to think more of herself and she couldn't regret that. He'd shown her how to embrace her sensuality and make a man fall apart in her arms and she'd never regret that. He'd stolen her heart, and that was unfortunate given that he didn't seem to want it, but at least now she knew love in all its passionate, painful brightness.

And she refused to regret that.

Only the wearing of the ring had been a mistake, and that was easily fixed. All she had to do was take it off.

Word came with breakfast that Theo's helicopter would be at her disposal from nine a.m. onwards. Aury received the message in silence and Moriana acknowledged it with a cool nod. Only when Moriana bade the guards to leave the room and shut the door behind them did her brittle façade drop. She'd been hoping Theo would come for her this morning, ask to see her, maybe even be contrite when it came to their harsh words spoken last night. She wanted him to fight for her love. He was a fighter, was he not? A master strategist who knew what everyone else at the table wanted?

She guessed not.

She took the ring off and set it on the table and Aury looked at it and sighed. 'So that's it?'

Moriana nodded, not trusting herself to speak.

'You could talk to him,' Aury suggested carefully.

'I have talked.' And loved, and given him her all and discovered herself stronger for it. 'Marriages are built on trust and Theo trusts no one. I'm worth more than he's offering and I don't want to compromise.'

'Good for you.' But Aury looked as miserable and uncertain as Moriana felt. 'His loss.'

A knock on the door drew their attention—and Moriana's hope—but it was only the newspapers for the day and she sent them away unread.

'I've grown,' she told the uncharacteristically silent Aury.

'I'll say.'

'For the better, I hope.'

'Definitely for the better.' Aury smiled and it was small but genuine. 'So, this foreign palace for a week was adequate but ultimately unsatisfying.' She waved her hand dismissively at the chandeliers and the light streaming in through gauze-curtained windows. 'We can do far better than this. Perhaps somewhere with more sunshine and fewer kings.'

'I think perhaps the south of France.' Moriana could get behind that. 'Sun, fun and healing.'

'Please let there also be retail therapy,' added Aury.

'There can be. I'll sell a painting.'

'We could go there directly.' Aury never complained of rapid changes in plans; she embraced them. 'It would take one phone call to get the villa up and running.'

'Do it.' Maybe there could even be hedonism and debauchery and falling in love all over again with someone new.

Doubtful, but still... Better than thinking she was going there to mourn the loss of a future that would have been a perfect fit.

Had Theo loved her.

'Pack light for us both and have Sam send the rest back to Arun.' There was no point staying where she wasn't wanted. 'We leave at half nine.' Long enough to pen thank you notes for the staff who had attended her so well during her stay. Long enough to draw up a plan for exhibiting those heritage gowns and to hand it over to Letitia, who might see it done.

'Good plan,' said Aury. 'Consider it done. Would you like me to call Arun and let them know?'

'Yes, but I don't want to talk to anyone.' She couldn't deal with speaking to either Augustus or her father right now. She had no strength left for flippant defences or breezy reassurances. 'If Augustus wants to talk, he can call Theo. Tell them I'm busy seducing the unwary and I'll call once we get to France and I have a spare moment.'

'You do realise your brother will have a fit when he learns the engagement is off?' Aury warned.

'His choice.' Moriana tried to shrug off her guilt at disappointing her family and almost succeeded. 'I tried to fit in here and didn't succeed. I hurt, I bleed, I make mistakes and love unwisely. No one's perfect and I'm through with trying to be. I'm me. And they can take me or leave me.'

Theo handed Moriana into the helicopter and tried not to let his terror show. This past week had been more intense than he ever could have imagined. Laughter and luxury, anguish and self-loathing, argument and unbearable intimacy—he'd been bombarded by emotion, and he still hadn't told Moriana how much she meant to him.

Oh, he'd shown it in a thousand wordless ways but Moriana didn't speak the language he'd perfected back when there was no one to talk to and no one he could trust and the only way to show favour was by deed. He could have trusted Benedict, had he known then what he knew now, but he hadn't, and that was a stain on his conscience that was destined to spread. He trusted Moriana more than he'd ever trusted anyone, and he loved her beyond measure, but he couldn't find the words, and here he was putting her into a helicopter similar to the one that had taken his family and all he could think was *Never again*. He couldn't go through that again.

They'd travelled from palace to palace by helicopter to get here but that was different. He'd been going with her then. He wasn't the one on the ground about to look skyward.

'Don't go.'

She either hadn't heard him above the noise of the rotor blades or she didn't understand. He leaned closer, caught her arm and figured he must look like a madman. 'Go by car, by train, by damn horse—anything but this. My family died like this and my uncle arranged it. Don't leave in a helicopter. I can't stand it. I can't lose you too.'

He saw her eyes, dark and startled. And then she was out of the helicopter and tilting forward as she strode towards the castle, turning when within safe distance to draw a line across her throat for anyone watching. *This flight wasn't happening, cut the engine, stand down, at ease.*

He'd never felt less at ease.

He strode from the courtyard, Moriana silent at his side, keeping pace with him but only just. They passed Sam, who stood at the doorway but she chose not to make eye contact and neither did any of his security detail. Good call. What could he tell them that they didn't already know? The Princess wasn't leaving as arranged.

He kept his silence as they walked to his rooms. Moriana kept her confusion to herself, faltering only when they were away from prying ears and eyes and he'd shut the door behind them.

When he turned back around she stood by the fireplace, hands clasped in front of her and her stance so regal and assured that he knew she was quailing inside.

'What was that?'

That was him, trying to makc things right with her, only it was entirely possible that he needed to do some more explaining. 'I didn't want you to go. Not like that.'

'Your office organised that flight. *You* authorised it.' Her voice held a hint of disbelief.

'I know. I changed my mind. I had a flashback to the day my family died and… I may have lost faith in helicopter travel. A little.'

There was no objection from her there.

'Your uncle did what?' she asked tentatively.

Theo pocketed his hands and nodded. It was now or never, and never wasn't an option with this woman. 'The day my family died I was meant to be on that helicopter too. The trip had been planned as a family outing, but I was wilder then and not always inclined to obey my parents. Benedict had turned up and talked me into going to the races with him. Fortune had favoured me—that's what they said. I had a bad case of survivor guilt—that's what Benedict said. It wasn't until years later that the information came to light that the helicopter had been tampered with and my uncle was behind it. He wanted the throne. He'd have kept it if not for me.'

'And do you think this helicopter has been tampered with too?'

'No. Nothing like that.' He'd been standing there, watching her leave, and fear had snaked into him and squeezed. 'But all of a sudden I couldn't stand to watch you leave in one. My uncle's gone. Benedict's gone. I've only just claimed you and you were leaving too. I couldn't let you.'

He wanted her to talk now, to gently guide him, to be his muse but she stayed silent.

'I always assumed that Benedict had known of his father's plans and had…saved me…or something. I realised yesterday that Benedict knew nothing. He just wanted someone to go to the races with. When Benedict realised what his father had done, and that I'd thought him complicit, he disavowed us both. Who could blame him? But it made me realise that I should have trusted him. I could have talked to him more, not kept everything to myself. That's not a mistake I want to make with you. I trust you. I need you to know what I think of you.'

'Go on,' she said warily, looking for all the world as

if she expected him to list a dozen faults in minute detail, but that wasn't where he was going with this at all.

'You think I don't know how to love you but I do,' he began. 'You don't know whether I enjoyed this past week or not but it's the best week I've ever had, and as for the sex…the sex is incandescent. I don't get lost in it the way I used to but that's only because there's never a moment when I can't see you and feel you and want you. That connection to you means everything to me. I want you at my side more than ever and I've wanted *that* since I was fourteen years old.' He took a deep breath and ploughed on. 'I love you and never want to lose you the way I've lost so many others, and sometimes that's going to mean that I haul you off a helicopter for no good reason other than I'm scared.'

'You love me?'

'So much. And I would spend my life trying to make you happy and proud of me, and maybe sometimes you'd have to poke and prod before I let you into my thoughts, but I'd do it. For you I'd do it. For us. And I know I've never asked properly, but I'm asking it of you now. Please will you marry me?'

She ventured forward, tentatively at first, but by the time she reached for his tie and wound it around her fist and reeled him in she was smiling. 'I'm going to hold you to the sharing part, and the loving part. And the having fun. And there should definitely be more lessons. Yes, I'll marry you,' she said, and kissed him and it felt like coming home.

'I'll drive you to Arun later,' he promised. 'Or we'll both go by helicopter. Okay?'

'I'm a little busy here.' Unbuttoning his shirt, yes. Why wasn't he *helping* with that? 'We should travel to Arun tomorrow.'

'We *should*.' She'd discovered his belt buckle and his rapidly rising appreciation.

'I have a form letter to write today,' she continued as she took him in hand. '*I, Moriana, the almost Perfect, take you, Theo, the mostly Magnificent*—this is where you write your name—*to have and to hold and never let go. Know that when you place your trust in me I will never let you down or give you cause to doubt my allegiance. You're mine and I'm yours and with you at my side I feel invincible*.' She smiled and he was powerless to stop himself pressing his lips to that generous curve. 'That should worry you.'

'It doesn't,' he murmured, with a kiss for the dimple at the corner of that smile.

'I'll make you proud.'

'You always do.' She didn't know her own worth but he had a lifetime in which to convince her of it. 'You make me strong.'

'You've always been that.'

'Not always.' Sometimes he'd been lost. 'I've never been surer of anyone. I've never been more prepared to make a spectacle of myself in pursuit of you. I love you.'

She lifted her hand to his cheek and brought her forehead to his. 'I love you too.'

CHAPTER ELEVEN

MORIANA LOOKED IN the gilt-edged mirror and a royal bride stared back at her. The gown glowed with a faint ivory sheen, the bodice and waist crafted to fit and the skirt flaring gently to flow like water when she walked. Her tiara glittered with centuries-old Arunian diamonds and her veil was currently pushed back to show her face. Today was the day and although Letitia fussed and Aury sighed, Moriana had never missed her mother more.

It was four weeks to the day since Theo had buried his uncle, with full State Honours. Three weeks and six days since Theo and Benedict had settled their differences by getting royally drunk after the funeral and facing off against each other in the palace vegetable garden, wielding antique swords and shields that neither of them could lift and wearing helmets that rendered them blinder than they already were.

They'd been aided in their reconciliation efforts by their capable and significantly less inebriated seconds, namely one Princess Moriana of Arun, who stood for the King, and commoner Enrique Cordova, who stood for Prince Benedict. Moriana liked Enrique—he balanced Benedict's acerbic wit and volatile disposition with dry good humour and unshakeable calm.

Theo had knighted Enrique just prior to the duel, although to what Order was anyone's guess. No one remembered the finer points.

What Moriana did remember was Benedict and Theo stretched out on the ground staring at the sky and ragged words dredged from somewhere deep within both of them.

Words like, 'I still love him, even though I hate him for what he did.'

Words like, 'You could stay on. You and your Knight.'

By morning Theo had a best man and Benedict had his cousin back. In the past weeks they'd reconnected and Liesendaach had loudly rejoiced that the rift that had come between the two cousins these past years had been mended.

Long live antique swords, alcohol and forgiveness.

If Theo had Benedict at his side today, Moriana had Aury—who would not stop nervously double-guessing the stylists and dressers until forced to desist by the ever-wise Letitia. The older woman took control, and by the time they were ready to leave for the cathedral both bride and bridesmaid looked their absolute best.

The spectacle that greeted them as they stepped from the palace and headed for the closed bridal carriage made the breath catch in her throat. She'd grown used to having a mounted guard these past three weeks as she'd journeyed from Arun's palace to Liesendaach's. She and three hundred of Arun's finest black warhorses had been met at the border of the two countries by three hundred of Liesendaach's matching greys—and then all six hundred mounted guards had accompanied her the rest of the way, with the big greys leading the way and the black steeds protecting the rear.

A circus had nothing on the last three weeks of travel. On the jousting and melee demonstrations the horsemen put on each evening for the gathering crowds. On the way Theo often turned up at the end of the day and rode with her for the last hour so that when they stopped he could help her from her horse and lavish her with a meal provided by a local hotelier or innkeeper.

Today, though, the mounted guards had opted for a different formation. The six steeds pulling the carriage were all black, but the rest of the guards had formed in groups of four. Grey, black, black, grey—two countries entwined and stronger for it.

She had all of this and at the end of the day she would have a man who worshipped her body and kept her warm and looked at her as if she hung the moon.

It was two hours to the cathedral, with the horses moving at a fast walk. They'd debated taking a car instead but Moriana had insisted that tradition be upheld. They had water in the carriage and biscuits that would leave no stain if dropped on clothes. They had a computer and could watch the procession on the news, and wasn't that a surreal experience? Watching an aerial view of the crowds lining the streets, and the horses and her father and brother at the head of the guard coming into view, being talked about in glowing terms, and then seeing the carriage come into view and knowing she was *in* the carriage.

She watched as various guests made their way into the cathedral. Watched as Theo and Benedict arrived by Bentley and smiled and joked as they strode up the steps, only for the cathedral to then swallow them too.

The press were being more than kind to Moriana today—it seemed she could do no wrong. From her choice of wedding gown, courtesy of the coffers of Liesendaach's costume collection, to the clear happiness of King Theodosius—every wedding choice she'd made had been celebrated and embraced.

The old Moriana would have revelled in the honeymoon period with the press. The new Moriana had been too damn *happy* to give it more than a passing thought.

And then it was time to touch up her make-up and bring the veil down over her face, and to take her bouquet of white roses from their storage place and let Aury alight before her to pave the way for Moriana's appearance.

With her father on one side and her brother on the other, she stepped out of the carriage and into first her father's arms and then her brother's.

'Do you feel loved yet?' Augustus asked drily, because as far as he was concerned the past three weeks had been one long, loving, expensive farewell. 'Or would you like even more adulation?'

'You can tell me I'd make our mother proud of me today and that you're going to miss me like crazy,' she suggested, and blinked back sudden tears when her ultra-reserved brother did exactly that.

The veil brushed her face as Aury made last-minute adjustments to its fall. Finally the flowers, veil, the train of her gown, *everything* was perfect as Moriana started up the stairs on her father's arm. They stopped at the cathedral doors and waited for the signal to continue.

Moriana had practised for this moment. In the flesh and in her head, more times than she could count. But nothing had prepared her for the roar of the crowd and the butterflies in her heart as the bishop appeared and beckoned them inside.

'Are you ready?' asked her father quietly.

'I love him.'

'Then you're ready.'

She didn't remember how she walked up that aisle, only that the choir sounded like angels and the ceiling soared and light shone down on everyone from behind stained glass windows and not for a moment did she falter. Theo was waiting for her, Theo was there, in full black military uniform, weighed down with military braid, medals and insignias. He was every inch the royal figurehead, and then he turned to her and smiled and it was wicked and ever so slightly sweet, and *there* was the man she wanted to spend the rest of her life with.

She remembered very little of kneeling and taking her vows. She did remember the ring sliding onto her finger and sliding a similar ring onto Theo's finger and she definitely remembered the lifting of her veil and the wonder in Theo's eyes as he kissed her.

'You're mine now.' His hands trembled in hers and she was grateful for that tiny show of frailty, just for her. It matched her own.

'I really am. For the rest of our lives.'

'I love you,' he whispered as they turned to face the congregation and beyond. 'And I'm yours.'

* * * * *

LET'S TALK

Romance

For exclusive extracts, competitions
and special offers, find us online:

f facebook.com/millsandboon

⊙ @millsandboonuk

🐦 @millsandboon

Or get in touch on 0844 844 1351*

For all the latest titles coming soon,
visit millsandboon.co.uk/nextmonth

Want even more
ROMANCE?

Join our bookclub today!

'Mills & Boon books, the perfect way to escape for an hour or so.'

Miss W. Dyer

'Excellent service, promptly delivered and very good subscription choices.'

Miss A. Pearson

'You get fantastic special offers and the chance to get books before they hit the shops'

Mrs V. Hall

Visit millsandbook.co.uk/Bookclub and save on brand new books.

MILLS & BOON